PETE JOHNSON

THE BAD SPY'S GUIDE

CORGI YEARLING BOOKS

THE BAD SPY'S GUIDE
A CORGI YEARLING BOOK 978 0 440 86763 0

Published in Great Britain by Corgi Yearling,
an imprint of Random House Children's Books

This edition published 2007

5 7 9 10 8 6 4

Set in 14/15.5pt Century Schoolbook by
Falcon Oast Graphic Art Ltd.

Corgi Yearling Books are published by
Random House Children's Books,
61–63 Uxbridge Road, London W5 5SA

www.**kids**at**randomhouse**.co.uk

Addresses for companies within the Random House Group Limited can
be found at: www.randomhouse.co.uk/offices.htm

THE RANDOM HOUSE GROUP Limited Reg. No. 954009

A CIP catalogue record for this book is available from the
British Library.

Printed in the UK by CPI Bookmarque, Croydon, CR0 4TD

'Henry,' I cried eagerly, 'you can trust me, you know. Just tell me why you're spying on the Baxters.'

'I'm not,' he said, breathing deeply. 'Got to go now,' he added, getting up and rushing to the door.

'Don't forget your glasses,' I called. And just to try and lighten the atmosphere because it had got incredibly tense, I slipped them on for a second. I expected not to be able to see a thing and to make a little joke. Actually, I could see through them perfectly.

I handed them to him, greatly puzzled. 'These aren't real glasses, are they?'

He looked at me. 'No.'

'So why wear glasses when you don't need to . . . ? It doesn't make any sense.' I paused. 'Unless you're trying to disguise yourself. Is that what you're doing?'

'Yes,' he whispered, 'that's exactly what I'm doing . . .'

How many Pete Johnson books have you read?

Comedies:

HELP! I'M A CLASSROOM GAMBLER
'A real romp of a read that will leave readers
ravenous for more' *Achuka*

HOW TO TRAIN YOUR PARENTS
'Makes you laugh out loud' *Sunday Times*

TRUST ME, I'M A TROUBLEMAKER
*Winner of the 2006 Calderdale Children's Book of the Year
(Upper Primary)*
'The devastatingly funny Pete Johnson' *Sunday Times*

RESCUING DAD
'Most buoyant, funny and optimistic' *Carousel*

Thrillers:

AVENGER
*Winner of the 2005 Sheffield Children's Book Award,
Children's Books shorter novel*
'A brilliant read' *Sunday Express*

THE CREEPER
'Readers will love it' *The Bookseller*

THE FRIGHTENERS
'Prepare to be thoroughly spooked' *Daily Mail*

THE GHOST DOG
Winner of the 1997 Young Telegraph / Fully Booked Award
'Incredibly enjoyable' *Books for Keeps*

TRAITOR
'Fast paced and energetic' *The Bookseller*

Including: MY FRIEND'S A WEREWOLF and
THE PHANTOM THIEF

This story is dedicated to Peter Coke,
with grateful thanks for bringing radio's
greatest ever detective – Paul Temple –
so brilliantly to life.

Chapter One

One tatty ID card.

That's all I've got left of the most incredible tale you'll ever hear. Still, you've never seen an ID card like this one before. 'A passport into another far more brilliant world.' That's what I said when I first saw it.

By the way, the ID card isn't actually mine. No, it belongs to a boy called Henry. And it all started one swelteringly hot night in June . . .

No, stop. I'm rushing into the story far too quickly. I'm dead keen, you see. But first things first.

My name is Tasha (no one, not even any of my teachers, calls me Natasha), I'm twelve years old and I want to be a private investigator. The first time I mentioned this everyone killed themselves laughing and thought, she'll grow out of it. But I haven't!

In fact, I've even had some training. How did I manage that? Well, take a peek in my bedroom. There you'll see eight shelves crammed with mystery stories. You won't just find the ones people in my class are reading either. No, there are dead old ones too: like James Bond and every Sherlock Holmes story ever written.

But I didn't just read them. I studied them. I learned from them. You could say I've been trained by the very best.

I only had one tiny problem. I didn't have any mysteries to solve. Here I was, with all this training and enthusiasm . . . and nothing to do. Talk about frustrating.

I live in a sleepy little village called Little Farthingwell (or Little Fartingwell, as some people in my class prefer to call it), but in so many books I've read these are the very places that are just brimming with crime. So I've kept my eyes permanently peeled – and yes, all right, let's get this out of the way right now: I've made a few mistakes, including a real whopper recently.

I won't waste your time by going into all the details. I'll just say – well, the dentist's wife really did seem to just vanish and then a dog did keep sniffing around a part of the garden where she could so easily have been buried.

And yes, OK – it must have been quite a shock for that dentist to see me digging up his front garden at half past two in the morning. And I don't even blame him for calling the police, especially when his wife was away in— But you really don't want to hear any more about that, do you? Good – because I'm so sick of everyone going on and on about it.

Anyway, that's the thing about school: be just a little bit different (like me) and people don't like it, you know. And after that incident they came up to me at school saying I was mad and crazy – and a big joke. Only one person stuck up for me – and that was Julia, my best friend. But even she had a go at me in private.

I tell you, my image was in shreds. But

I wasn't going to stop. And on a slightly happier note I did go on to find this suitcase by the side of the road. It was locked and I had such high hopes that it had been dropped by bank robbers and was full of stolen money. In fact, it was full of smelly clothes and had just fallen off a car roofrack. No, wait, I did get a little reward for discovering it – so it was a start, I suppose.

All the time, though, I was waiting for that big mystery where I could show off all my investigating skills . . . and now I really can take you on to that swelteringly hot night in June when I finally got my chance.

Chapter Two

On the evening I'm telling you about, I was on my own for a few hours because Dad was driving my mum to the airport. She was flying off to New York – swanky or what – where she would travel about for the next three weeks telling everyone why she was a top businesswoman. I was proud of her. But right then the house had a horrible, empty feeling which I didn't like at all.

And normally I'd have been on the phone to Julia. But she'd gone down with such a bad attack of summer flu she could hardly speak; her mum thought it best I didn't even text her right now and just let her have complete rest.

My room was so stuffy that night, I opened my bedroom window wide. But all the new air felt as worn out and tired as the old stuff. Everything was just so flat. If only someone would call round with a mystery for me to solve. People were always dropping in on Sherlock Holmes. Surely one person could consult me. They needn't pay me a penny either. In fact I'd pay them! That's how desperate I was.

There must be someone out there who needed my help.

And that's when I spotted a figure crouched underneath the massive cherry tree in our front garden. Immediately I reached for my notebook, which goes absolutely everywhere with me.

Then the person beneath our cherry tree sprang forward – and I recognized him. He caught the same bus as Julia and me every morning – and went to the boys' school just down the road from our concentration camp. He was called Henry Grimes; he'd only been in the village a short while and Julia thought he was a geek. I'd met him once when I was out with Mum at the shops. She had stopped to chat to his mum when they first moved in. All I'd noticed about Henry's mum, actually, was that she had striking red hair (you see, I'm very observant, like all spies have to be).

Henry himself was quite tall and sliced-bread thin. He looked younger than his age (twelve) – a bit baby-faced really, with blond hair (Julia reckoned it was dyed) and glasses. When he took his glasses off, though, he had interesting eyes: they were a light green colour and always had a far-away look in them, as if he'd just landed here from a distant planet.

No, I'm not saying he was an alien. Behave! I'm just trying to explain that there was something a bit mysterious about him right from the start. I remember once I saw him on the bus sitting by himself and he intrigued me so much I very nearly went and sat next to him. I would have done if I hadn't been with Julia.

He lived in one of those cottages at the other end of the village, yet here he was hiding underneath the branches of our cherry tree. Why? I was just brimming with nosiness, especially when he got out a notebook and started scribbling furiously in it.

He appeared to be staring at the house opposite mine. A pair of prune-faced snobs called Mr and Mrs Baxter lived there. But I couldn't see what was so fascinating about it.

Finally he came out from under the cherry tree. He stood in the middle of the road, putting his notebook away and gazing at the Baxter abode as if he just couldn't tear his eyes away from it.

And then I yelled down to him, 'Hey, Henry, just what are you doing?'

He whirled round and he looked dead guilty, as if I'd caught him doing something really bad. Then he sort of gasped my name – 'Tasha!' – and never said another word. Well, the poor guy didn't get a chance, did he? For at the same moment a very old, very battered car came roaring down my road at a colossal speed. I could see the driver wrestling frantically with the controls. Then the car gave a tremendous swerve and backfired so loudly, it sounded just like a gunshot.

And there – sprawled on the ground and lying very still – was Henry.

Chapter Three

I hared down my stairs. It had all happened in a flash, so I hadn't even been able to shout a warning to Henry.

I flew outside, where to my huge relief, I saw Henry sitting up and talking to the older boy who'd been driving the car.

Henry suddenly noticed me and gave a tiny smile. 'Hello again . . . we got interrupted, didn't we?'

'Are you hurt anywhere?' I asked.

'No he's not, says he feels fine,' cried the driver hastily.

'Don't think there's anything broken anyway,' said Henry. 'Not even my glasses.'

He put them on again. 'So I've been pretty lucky really. I jumped out of the way just in time.' He looked as pale as milk, though, and he got to his feet so gingerly.

The driver started talking to Henry again, saying how he'd only passed his test two days ago and he didn't want anything going on his licence. That was all he was bothered about. Then I noticed Henry's little notebook and pen had flown down the road, so I picked them up.

And his notebook was exactly like mine. So that was one thing – probably the only one – that he and I had in common: an identical taste in notebooks. I slipped it into my pocket.

Henry shook hands with the driver, who was all smiles now he knew Henry wasn't going to report the accident. Neighbours were hovering round too, with shocked, curious eyes, but I steered Henry away from them and into my house for a cup of tea.

Then, in the kitchen, I said to Henry, 'So come on, why have you been hanging about outside in such a highly suspicious manner?'

He took a slug of tea and then replied, 'Because we're living in exciting times,

Tasha.'

'Tell me more,' I cried at once.

'Do you know what's going on across the road?'

'No.'

'Well, an incredible thing has just occurred there.'

My skin was starting to sizzle now. 'You don't mean a crime?'

'No, I mean they've got a nest of goldfinches in their back garden.' Then, because I looked totally underwhelmed, he went on, 'I doubt you've ever seen a goldfinch before. They disappeared from our gardens years ago . . . but now suddenly they're back – at your neighbours' house. There was a bit about it in the village magazine last week.'

'Oh, was there?' I said vaguely.

'Well, do look out for goldfinches flying about. They've got a red and white face and a gold bar on their wings. They've also got a very distinctive cry. Perhaps you've heard it.' And right there in the kitchen he went: *'Twit, twit . . . twit, twit.'*

'Whenever I hear a bird going *twit twit*, I'll think of you,' I said. 'Do that again, will you?'

He started another impression, but then reddened. 'You're laughing at me, aren't you? That's cool, I do get carried away when I'm talking about goldfinches. They're such amazing birds. But I'll stop boring you now . . . and thanks for the tea. See you then.'

'Oh, before you go,' I said, 'I picked up your notebook.' I took it out of my pocket and handed it to him.

'Thanks a lot,' he cried, grabbing it eagerly. 'I've jotted down so many details about goldfinches in there. I saw one fly right above my head tonight. Bird-watchers all over the country are going to be so envious.'

'Remind me about that noise goldfinches make again.'

He grinned. 'You'll just have to remember my terrible impression. Bye.'

And off he went.

A nice, geeky bird-watcher – that's what you're thinking. Well, so was I until I realized I'd mixed up the notebooks and given Henry mine by mistake.

I was just quickly glancing through it when I got a shock. For he hadn't written down one single thing in it about goldfinches. Instead, there were all these notes about people who'd called on the Baxters: times they'd arrived, brief descriptions. The kind of reports you'd expect an undercover policeman to make.

But why was Henry doing this? And why did he pretend he was just observing goldfinches?

This needed investigating, didn't it?

Chapter Four

That night I sat down and read three Sherlock Holmes stories, including *A Case of Identity* – one of my top favourites. But I wasn't just reading for enjoyment. No, this was my way of sharpening up my detective skills.

And afterwards, I knew what I had to do. On the bus tomorrow I'd go up to Henry and say: 'I see our notebooks got mixed up last night.' Then I'd smile one of my knowing smiles. That should be enough to break him down.

Just to be sure, I practised my knowing smile in the mirror for a few minutes.

I'm very professional like that. When I'm on a case, nothing is too much trouble.

The following morning – knowing smile at the ready – I waited for Henry at the bus stop. He never turned up. He wasn't on the bus home either. His behaviour was now looking highly suspicious. And I was getting more and more intrigued.

But what should I do next? Go round to his house and confront him? It was Friday, so I wouldn't normally see him again now until the bus on Monday morning. Could I wait that long?

I was still thinking about this when Mum rang from New York. She said to me, 'Now I'm only away for three weeks and while Dad's taken some time off work, I'm sure you two will have great fun together.'

She and Dad must have the same scriptwriter, because he keeps going on about how we're going to have 'great fun' as well. And nothing chills your blood more than when people keep saying that to you.

Anyway, just as Mum was ringing off she said, 'Do try and stay out of trouble, love.' Then she added, 'And I hope you enjoy going bowling with Leo.'

And do you know, I'd totally forgotten

that I was going on a kind of date that night. That was quite shocking actually, because Leo – who is a year older than me, and goes to the same boys' school as Henry – is dead fit and loads of girls at my school like him. Actually, he's taken quite a few girls bowling before me. But I was the first one from my form. So it was kind of an honour to be chosen and I had been looking forward to it. But the moment I have a mystery to solve, everything else just vanishes from my head – yes, even fit-looking boys.

I raced upstairs to get ready. Right on time, Leo rang the doorbell and Dad sprang out at him like a mad genie. He was wearing one of his tragic cardigans as well . . . Dad, that is, not Leo. And I thought, Dad's going to really interrogate this poor boy now and he'll run from the house screaming. But actually, Dad was twinkling like a Christmas tree and only let himself down right at the end when he called after us, 'Remember to look after my girl, won't you?' as if Leo were taking me to Mars.

I said at once, 'I apologize two million times for that.'

'No, I think it's kind of cute,' replied Leo, then with a grin he added: 'Like you.'

I went a tiny bit shivery then . . . any boy paying me a compliment always has that effect on me. And then Leo started telling me something funny – and by the time we reached the bowling alley I had a pain from laughing so much.

We had a good time that evening. I even won the bowling – and Leo didn't mind at all. (Later I found out he always lets the girl win.) And when he asked me with one of his cheeky grins: 'So will you go out with me again?' I said, 'I just might.' I knew I had to play it cool. But actually, I did like him. I'd have liked him even more if he needed saving from a criminal mastermind – but you can't have everything, can you? And I floated into my house, where Dad was sitting in the kitchen.

'Enjoy yourself?' he asked – a bit crisply, I thought. I sat down opposite him.

'Yes, it was great. I won the bowling and Leo didn't mind at all. Is everything all right?' I added.

Dad swallowed. 'Well, another young man was here tonight, eager for your company.'

My chair hit the wall behind me as I leaped up. 'Was it Henry?' I cried eagerly.

Dad nodded slowly.

'But he's the boy I told you about; the one who nearly got run over right outside our house.'

'Well, he's coming round again tomorrow afternoon, about two o'clock.'

'Oh brilliant,' I cried, but seeing Dad's eyes grow even wider, I added hastily, 'I'm just so keen to know how his health is, after the accident.'

Then I shot upstairs. So tomorrow afternoon would be my chance to crack this mystery. But how? I decided a knowing smile just wouldn't be enough. Then I wondered what Sherlock Holmes would do at a moment like this – and inspiration hit me.

Sherlock Holmes would set out to break Henry's cover story, wouldn't he? Prove he wasn't really a bird-watcher at all. Then, his cover demolished, Henry would have no choice but to tell me the truth. Well, I would do exactly the same.

As soon as I got up the following morning, I spent an hour and a half on the internet

– and at the end I had compiled a whole list of tough questions on goldfinches.

At two o'clock, I saw Henry stroll – rather nervously, I felt – up to my house. Luckily Dad was in the back garden painting the garage; he had said he wanted to get on with some DIY while Mum was away. So we shouldn't be disturbed. I sprang downstairs just as Henry rang the doorbell.

'I'm back again,' he grinned.

Anyone else looking at him would just see a tallish, shy twelve-year-old. But right then I just knew he had a secret. I could sense it. It was like a scent in the air.

'I think our notebooks got mixed up,' he said.

I nodded and said, 'We'll swap upstairs.'

He looked a little surprised at this, but then he limped after me. He said his right leg was still painful after the accident and he hadn't gone to school yesterday. So I supposed that explained why he wasn't on the bus.

He immediately started looking at all my mystery books. He read out some of the titles: '*Casino Royale, Paul Temple and the Tyler Mystery, The Thirty-Nine Steps.*

This is an amazing collection – the best I've ever seen. Why, you've even got—'

'Do you want to sit down?' I interrupted. I was all strung up and eager for my cross-examination to begin. He lowered himself into a chair but I continued pacing around. 'How long have you been bird-watching then, Henry?' I asked.

'Can't remember a time when I wasn't,' he replied. 'They've always fascinated me.'

'And the goldfinch is a special favourite?'

'It sure is.'

'And how many eggs does it lay?' I asked.

'How many eggs?' he repeated.

'Yes.'

'Well . . . it's just a couple.'

'And what colour are the eggs?'

'They're white – why do you ask?'

I ignored this question. 'And the goldfinch isn't the only bird to have vanished from our gardens, is it? What are some of the others?'

'Now let me have a think about that . . .' Henry took off his glasses, and then shook his head. 'Sorry, it's gone.'

'Skylarks, yellowhammers and wood warblers are three . . .'

'Oh, yes, that's right,' he said, nodding. 'My head went blank for a minute there.'

'And by the way, Henry, the goldfinch lays between four and six eggs, not two – and they're not white either, they're cream-coloured and spotted with red-brown.'

He slipped lower in his chair. 'I had no idea you knew so much about birds.'

I didn't answer, just threw in one of my knowing smiles. Well, I had been practising it for days. Then I cried, 'We'd better swap notebooks now.'

After we'd done that I announced, 'Just got to pop to the bathroom.' I moved off noisily but then crept back again to watch Henry's actions through a crack in the door. I was not disappointed either.

He was only staring at his notebook through a magnifying glass! In an instant I knew what he was doing. He was searching the pages for fingerprints. He needed to know exactly what I'd seen.

This was very odd behaviour indeed. A wave of joy quivered through me. I had a real mystery to solve all right. Then I let out a gasp.

Someone had just touched my left shoulder.

Chapter Five

I slowly turned round to face . . . my dad.
I'd never even heard him come upstairs.
Now he was gazing at me in complete
bewilderment.

'Oh, hi, Dad,' I squeaked.

'What on earth are you doing?'

I could feel this gigantic blush sweeping
across my face. 'Oh, just having a look at
what Henry is up to,' I whispered. 'That's
the boy who had the accident. You spoke to
him yesterday. Now he's just popped
into my room . . . and I'm having a little look
at him.' I smiled as confidently as I could at
Dad, whose eyes were enormous now.

'But why are you whispering . . . is this some kind of game?'

'Yes, Dad,' I said quickly, 'that's exactly what it is – I'll teach you how to play it one day.'

Then, very fortunately, the phone rang.

Dad rushed downstairs while I shot back into my bedroom. In one swift movement Henry had slipped the magnifying glass away.

He said to me, 'I expect you had a little peek inside my notebook. Well, you had to do that otherwise you wouldn't have known it wasn't yours, would you? And just in case you were wondering why there was nothing about goldfinches in it – I was waiting to spot one of them. And while I was waiting I just wrote a load of gibberish down, doesn't mean a thing.' He was speaking very quickly, and was that sweat glistening on his forehead? I felt kind of sorry for him. But I was working on a case which had to be solved.

'I'm afraid,' I said sternly, 'I don't believe you're a bird-watcher at all. Well, you didn't even know the correct colour of goldfinches' eggs. Surely someone who pretended to love goldfinches as much as you would know that.'

He suddenly went very still, just the way dogs do when they think they're in trouble.

'No, I believe that was just your cover story. It was the Baxters you were really interested in.'

He tried to smile. 'Why would I be interested in them?'

'That's what I've been wondering.'

'Look, I hardly know you,' he cried, 'so I've got no right to ask you this – but will you please do me a big favour? Forget the notebook, forget we've spoken today.'

'Henry,' I cried eagerly, 'you can trust me, you know. Just tell me why you're spying on the Baxters.'

'I'm not,' he said, breathing deeply. 'Got to go now,' he added, getting up and rushing to the door.

'Don't forget your glasses,' I called. And just to try and lighten the atmosphere because it had got incredibly tense, I slipped them on for a second. I expected not to be able to see a thing and to make a little joke. Actually, I could see through them perfectly.

I handed them to him, greatly puzzled.
'These aren't real glasses, are they?'

He looked at me. 'No.'

'So why wear glasses when you don't
need to . . . ? It doesn't make any sense.' I
paused. 'Unless you're trying to disguise
yourself. Is that what you're doing?'

'Yes,' he whispered, looking thoroughly
miserable, 'that's exactly what I'm doing.'

'But why?'

He didn't answer at first, just got up and
roamed around my bedroom staring at my
books again. I didn't say a word; I sensed
if I just left him alone he would tell me the
truth. Then at last he hissed, 'All right,
I'm a junior investigative operator – also
known as a spy.'

I gaped at him. 'You? But you're too
young.'

'Children make the best spies of all for
that very reason. No one ever suspects
them.'

'That's true,' I murmured.

'But I've made one mistake after
another these past twenty-four hours . . .
and now I've told you my true identity.
Something we're never supposed to do.
You've been very clever tonight, especially

catching me out with those questions about goldfinches.'

'I've trained with the best,' I said, waving at my crime books. 'And don't worry, I'll help you all I can . . . but what exactly is going on?'

Before he could answer, Dad picked this of all moments to prance in with a tray of drinks.

'Well, I think some light refreshments are called for, especially on a hot afternoon like this,' he said cheerily.

But Henry looked suddenly very startled. 'That's really kind of you' – he was speaking in gulps now – 'but I'm already late for . . . for an appointment.' Then he hobbled down the stairs at an amazing speed, with me right after him.

'Don't go yet,' I said.

'I've been very foolish today,' said Henry. Then he whispered, 'Whoever knows my true identity could be in danger.'

'Oh, danger doesn't worry me,' I cried.

'But I must tell someone what I've done immediately . . . don't try and contact me . . . let me call you, please.'

'Oh, all right,' I said. I quickly tore a page out of my notebook and scribbled down my numbers: both home and mobile – I didn't want to take any chances! 'Call me any time. Any time at all. I'll be ready,' I said, handing them to Henry.

'I will come back . . . when I can,' he said, stuffing the paper into his pocket. Then, in a voice barely above a whisper, 'Tell no one what happened tonight. One stray word could jeopardize everything. And believe me, Tasha, this mission is piping hot!'

Before I could say anything else – or even ask for his number – Henry had bolted out of the door. Then I noticed Dad looming behind. He was downing one of the glasses of orange juice himself. 'Rather a shy chap, isn't he?' he murmured.

I just nodded. I didn't trust myself to speak to Dad right now. If he hadn't blundered in when he did, Henry would have told me everything.

Now I was just going to have to wait.

Chapter Six

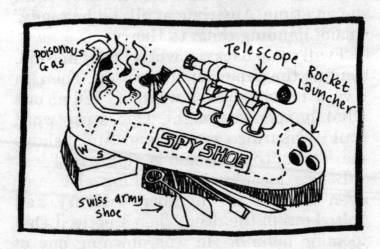

Poisonous Gas

Telescope

Rocket Launcher

SPY SHOE

W S

Swiss army shoe

Shortly after Henry left, I heard 'Hey, Snot-face' croaked down my mobile. It was Julia and she always calls me 'Snot-face' when she's feeling affectionate.

'You sound terrible,' I said.

'I feel even worse,' she began, and then had to stop for a coughing fit. 'Now I know what it feels like to be a hundred and three,' she gasped. 'Well, come on, cheer me up and tell me all the goss.'

How about, *Oh, I've just met a spy* . . . I was just dying to tell Julia that. But I'd been sworn to secrecy. So instead I told her about my date with Leo. I ended by saying,

'He wants to see me again . . . or so he said.'

'Leo'll see you again,' wheezed Julia, who lives quite near him. 'I have it on good authority that he thinks you're the most amazing thing to walk this planet. Now, has anything else happened?'

'Not a thing,' I said at once.

'Come on, you're keeping something from me.'

'No I'm not.'

'Oh yes you are, I can always tell – call it best friend's instinct,' said Julia. 'You're not planning on digging up any more people's gardens in the middle of the night, are you?'

'Ah, you never know where I might strike next: the phantom gardener.'

'That's what worries me . . . anyway, I'm off to have another coughing fit. What fun.'

'Well, hurry up and get better . . . for some odd reason, I miss you.'

'I sort of miss me too. Bye.'

Later, I carried on that conversation with Julia in my head. And I imagined what she'd have said if I had told her about Henry being a spy. I knew she'd have laughed a lot and been highly sceptical, because that's what Julia is like. She'd also have said: 'But where's his proof?'

And even though I'd discovered Henry's secret identity by my clever questioning, I supposed she was right there – I did need some proof.

There was something else I wondered about too. It was a really tiny point, but Henry had said his mission was 'piping hot'. Well, soup can be piping hot – but not a secret mission. That just isn't the language spies use. And I should know, because of all the books I've read.

Three highly frustrating days then passed without a word from Henry. He wasn't even on the bus on Monday or Tuesday. If I'd had his number, I don't think I could have resisted calling him. But then I remembered how emphatic he'd been about me not contacting him.

I did observe Mr Baxter walking past my window. Even on a blazing hot evening he was wearing a striped blue blazer that had been out of fashion for sixty years. He had a thin pinched face, with a very sharp nose, which made him look like a fierce eagle. And he always had this faint, self-satisfied smile on his face, like an eagle who'd just enjoyed a very good meal . . . Yes, I decided, he could very easily have a sinister secret. I couldn't wait to find out what it was.

And finally I saw Henry on the bus again. He whispered something so faintly I couldn't hear what he said. He'd started to move away until I hissed, 'Say that again.'

The next time I did just catch him saying, 'I'll be round about half past six tonight.'

Well, I got so excited, but then I told myself I must keep a clear head, just as Sherlock Holmes or James Bond would have done.

That night he had binoculars round his neck. 'Thought I'd better have these, just in case your dad or anyone wonders why I'm here. I can use the bird-watching cover again and it will give me a reason to be seen looking out of the window.' I was impressed. Those binoculars were a good touch – just the kind of thing a real spy would have thought of. He added, 'After our last conversation I did some more research on goldfinches. I don't want anyone else breaking my cover – as you so expertly did.' Then he apologized for not calling me before, but he'd come over all dizzy at home on Sunday night and the doctor had said he was suffering from delayed shock. So he hadn't been allowed out for a couple of days.

'Since I last saw you,' he said as we stood facing each other in my bedroom, looking as if we were about to start dancing, 'a great deal has happened.' Then he stopped. 'Do you mind if I close your window? I know we might be a bit hot . . .'

'No, that's all right,' I said, rushing up and shutting the window.

'Sorry to be so fussy, but you can't be too careful . . . in fact, that's the first rule in the spy guide.'

I stared at him, fascinated and entranced by all this inside info, but I knew there was something I just had to ask him. 'Er, Henry, before we go any further . . .?'

'Yes?'

'I just wondered if you had something on your person to prove you really are a spy.'

Immediately his jaw dropped several

thousand feet. 'I don't look like a spy to you, do I?'

'Oh, it's not that.'

'To be honest, I don't think I'd ever have become a spy if it hadn't been for my mum and dad. You see, they're both in the spying game – as we call it.'

'Oh wow,' I gasped. 'And double wow.'

'They're really top ones as well. So of course, they were dead keen for me to follow a career in spying too.' He gave a rather bitter laugh. 'Most parents tell their children to work hard, don't they? Mine always say: "Spy hard."'

'So how long have you been a spy then?'

'Since I was four.'

'Four?' I echoed, disbelievingly.

'That's right. They couldn't send me on any really dangerous missions until I was five though . . . that's a joke, by the way.'

I quickly smiled.

'No, when you're four or five they're just testing your skills of observation, because that's what a lot of spying is: they tell you spies always have to walk in the shadows; they must see without being seen. Then when you're eleven you learn the business of surveillance. And I passed an exam in that.'

'Congratulations.'

'Only just scraped a pass, though. My mum and dad were hoping for a distinction.' He shook his head. 'Now, you wanted some ID.'

I felt embarrassed. 'Oh, just anything you've got handy.'

'I'll need to take my shoe off first.'

'Oh, will you?' I watched him remove his left shoe and then slide back the heel. Now, that was impressive.

But then he said, 'I'm left-handed so I keep forgetting my secret ID is always kept in my right shoe. Sorry about that.'

'No, I can see how it could be confusing.'

'It isn't confusing at all,' murmured Henry. 'It's me. I'm just a very bad spy: one mistake after another lately.' He slid back the heel of his right shoe. 'Ah, now we're in business.' And he handed me the tiniest compass I'd ever seen.

He said, 'That's just so you always know where you are. Never had to use it actually, but it's nice to know it's there.'

It looked completely useless to me.

'I'm supposed to have a little map in

here as well . . . now, I wonder where that's gone. Anyway, I do have this.' He gave a triumphant smile, as if he'd just hauled up precious stones from the deep. And he handed me a battered little ID card. On this was written his full name (his middle name is Stewart, if you're at all interested, which you probably aren't) and a number.

I examined it doubtfully. I could have made a better card in five minutes on my computer. 'Got anything else hidden in that shoe?' I asked.

'That's the lot,' he replied. 'Of course I can't actually carry something saying too much about me – that would be very dangerous.'

'Yeah, of course,' I said. And I could totally see that. Also, the fact that it looked so tatty and ordinary – well, that was a good thing, really. I mean, it was much more likely that spies – real spies – would have something very everyday as their ID card. All that flashy stuff was just for the movies.

He looked at me anxiously. 'I sense you're still not happy.'

'Oh no, I'm very happy.' And I was. For as Sherlock Holmes said: 'When you've examined all the other possibilities, whatever remains, however improbable, is the truth.' Well, I was sure he wasn't a loon. And if he was just pretending to be a spy, he'd make out he was a brilliant one, wouldn't he? But Henry kept pointing out all his mistakes and disappointments – which made it seem so much more realistic.

I looked again at his tatty little ID card. It looked like nothing but actually it was, as I said aloud, 'A passport into another far more brilliant world.'

Now, I've told you that last bit already. Remember? What you don't know is the way Henry looked after I said that.

I tell you, he just glowed. We both did for several seconds.

Finally he said, 'And now I've got some very exciting news for you.'

'Yes?' I urged.

'The other spy on this mission is the one who's posing as my mum . . .'

'So she's not your real mum then?'

'Oh no, my real parents are both hundreds of miles away. And my dad may be gone for years.' He looked kind of sad then – and I thought, my mum's only been away for a few days and already I'm missing her quite badly. What must it be like to not see your dad for a year or more? I suppose that's the tough side of having spies for parents.

He went on, 'My fake mother is the leader of this operation and I told her about me blurting out to you that I was a spy. She was not pleased at all at first. But now, and here's the really brilliant news—'

It was at that moment that a huge noise filled our ears: the doorbell ringing twice.

'Ignore it, Henry, and go on with what you were saying,' I cried.

But then it rang twice more. And it was highly distracting. I mean, when you're about to talk about spy missions the last thing you want is doorbells going off every five seconds.

So I said, 'Don't worry. I'll get rid of whoever it is.' I charged down the stairs, fully expecting it to be someone for Dad, who was still working away in the garden.

It was Leo.

'I just happened to be passing,' he grinned, 'and I thought, I know a nice girl who'll offer a weary traveller a cup of tea.' Then he gazed at me from under his long, dark eyelashes and the next thing I knew he was sitting in the kitchen.

I put the kettle on in a kind of trance, wondering how many more minutes would have to pass before I could politely chuck Leo out. I mean, I really didn't want to upset my brand-new boyfriend. On the other hand, I had a spy waiting for me upstairs.

So I gulped down the tea extremely quickly, hoping it might encourage Leo to do the same. I didn't even really listen to what he was saying – something about going to the cinema? And then, just to add to the evening's horror, Dad wandered in, his face and clothes smeared with paint.

He seemed chuffed to bits to see Leo. 'Oh, hello there, no, don't get up.' Then he started telling us all about painting the garage. How interesting . . . not. He turned to me. 'I wouldn't say no to a cup of tea, love.'

I nearly howled with frustration, but what could I do? There really was no way I could get out of this kitchen. I was completely trapped, and Dad was settling down for a long chat with Leo.

Then, just when I thought my life

couldn't get any worse, I heard footsteps coming down the stairs.

Dad nearly choked with shock. 'Who on earth's that?'

'Well, I'm not quite sure,' I said, as if the house was over-run with people. 'But I think it might be Henry.'

'Who's Henry?' demanded Leo at once.

I actually didn't need to answer that question because Dad had galloped out of the kitchen just as Henry had reached the bottom of the stairs and was sliding towards the door.

'Oh, are you going, Henry?' I asked.

He jumped. 'Yes, yes, I'm going,' he explained.

Leo frowned darkly at him while Dad's eyes looked as if they were about to burst out of their sockets.

'Henry has been watching for gold-finches,' I explained to no one in particular. 'There's a nest of them across the road. Any luck tonight, Henry?'

'Oh yes, I heard a goldfinch calling and then spotted two of them flying about and enjoying the sunshine.'

What a professional answer, I thought – just the kind a real spy would give.

'Well, don't feel you have to rush away,' I said to him. 'Stay and watch the goldfinches for longer, if you like.'

'No, I've got to go now.' At the door he whispered to me, 'I'll be in contact,' and then winked, which perhaps was a mistake, as we were being keenly watched by Leo and Dad at the time.

I turned to face them after Henry had gone. 'That boy's just mad about goldfinches,' I said, with what I hoped was a merry laugh.

'So I see,' muttered Leo. 'I'll see you on Friday to go to the cinema then.' He said this rather as a teacher might say he'd see you for detention.

'I'm looking forward to it already,' I replied, trying to remember what he had said earlier. Had I agreed to go to the cinema with him on Friday?

But Leo didn't reply, just went stropping off.

Dad was watching all this while chewing his lip in a thoughtful way. He said to me, 'Let's go back into the kitchen, shall we, love?'

He picked up his mug of tea and took a large swig, then leaned forward. 'Do you know, I was about your age, Tasha, when I started dating. There were two lasses I especially liked. They both had their charms, as they say.' He paused, lost for a moment in Dadland. 'And I couldn't decide between them, so do you know what I did?' He leaned forward. 'I tried to see them both.'

Then I knew why I was being subjected to this yarn from prehistoric times. 'Dad, I'm not—'

He raised a hand. 'Hang on, let me finish my tale,' he cried mock-indignantly. 'Now where was I? Oh yes, I tried to see these two lasses. But you know it really wasn't much fun. It also got very complicated. And in the end they found me out, and do you know what they did?'

'Worked out a rota?'

'No, they both dumped me. How about that?'

'That's the saddest story I've ever heard, Dad. But can I just explain something? Henry is not my boyfriend. We're just watching goldfinches together – that's all.'

Dad's eyes started expanding at an alarming rate again. 'We'll talk about this again later,' he said. And a few minutes afterwards I heard him on the phone to Mum. He was saying, 'You've really got to help me. I'm totally out of my depth here.'

What a night!

And I still didn't know what Henry's exciting news was . . .

Chapter Seven

I had to wait another twenty-four hours for that. But it was worth waiting for.

Henry arrived in sunglasses, given to him by his bosses. 'They weren't too impressed with me getting run over, so now I've got these sunglasses which have mirrored edges built into the sides of the lenses, so you can see what's happening behind you.'

Of course I had to try them on. 'That's so brilliant as now you'll always know what people are doing behind your back.'

Henry went on, 'When I was given the

glasses I also told my bosses you were completely trustworthy and had exceptional detecting skills.'

'Oh, thank you.'

'And I mentioned how you've got an excellent view of the Baxters' house and your Tudor-style windows are perfect, because they're difficult to see into, but excellent for looking out of and so' – he paused, then grinned at me – 'they've decided your bedroom would make a perfect surveillance point for us.'

My bedroom, right in the centre of a major spy operation. Well, as moments go, this was just about the best ever.

I took a couple of deep breaths to control my excitement and asked, 'So why are we watching the Baxters?'

'First of all, I've got to explain a technical term: a sleeper—'

'That's someone who's recruited as an enemy agent,' I interrupted, 'but doesn't do anything for years. Instead, he spends all his time building up a really good cover.'

'Completely correct,' he said in an amazed voice. 'Well, we've had a tip-off that your neighbour, Mr Baxter, is a sleeper.'

'Excellent.'

'And he's recently been activated.'

'Even better.'

'We've been secretly monitoring him for weeks, noticing how he's been travelling about all over the place . . . and we believe he will, very shortly, pass over important secrets to our enemies. Well, what better setting for this transaction to take place than a quiet, peaceful village like Little Farthingwell?'

I gave a shiver of delight and asked, 'What about Mrs Baxter? Is she in on it too?'

'We think she must be,' said Henry. 'After all, she's going to have some very dodgy characters visiting her over the next few days. And we want to catch the lot. There's one guy we're especially keen to see: he's got a white beard and is absolutely massive – I could probably fit inside one of his trouser legs. They say he's also got bad breath like you wouldn't believe.'

'He sounds just lovely.'

'He's the key to it all, Tasha, and we're sure he's in this country. Under a false passport, of course.'

'Oh, of course,' I agreed.

'Now, he's dead tricky. If we could catch him that would be great, but if we could track him here with the Baxters – that would be fantastic.'

I looked at him. 'You're really enthusiastic about this mission, aren't you?'

'Well, I want to do something to make my mum and dad proud. I know I haven't yet. But this is my chance. So I really don't want to mess this up.'

'You won't. I won't let you,' I said.

He grinned. 'By the way, the man we're after has many different names but we call him "The Scorpion", because he is so treacherous. And in fact, this case is called Operation Scorpion.'

'And my bedroom will be the surveillance point for Operation Scorpion?'

'It will indeed.'

After that I had to get up and walk about a bit. This was like having five Christmases in one day. No wonder my head was spinning. And then, would you believe it, I got hiccups . . . this always happens to me at moments of excitement. I had a really bad attack when I was digging up the dentist's garden that night.

46

In fact, I think it was probably my hiccups that woke him up.

'Don't panic,' I cried. 'I'm just going to drink a glass of water and hold my nose – and don't you dare go home.' I shot off to the bathroom and swallowed a glass of water while at the same time holding my nose, then let out a burp you could hear fifty miles away. But the hiccups had gone.

I charged back. 'All sorted,' I said. 'Now tell me, are your bosses MI5?'

'Yeah, probably,' he said vaguely. 'We all work in small cells – for our own security – so I only know my immediate bosses, not the real high-ups.'

I said, 'One day you'll be one of the high-ups.'

He looked pleased. 'Do you think so?'

'I know it . . . you just needed that lucky break and now you've got it . . . meeting me.'

He smiled. 'By the way, we think the Scorpion might arrive one night this weekend.'

I nodded eagerly. Then I remembered something. 'The only thing is, I'm going to the cinema tomorrow with Leo. You met him yesterday. I expect you know him from school?'

'Not really . . . he's in the year above me.'

'But it's not a problem me going out tomorrow?'

'No, no,' he said quickly. 'We're not expecting any significant behaviour here tomorrow . . . it's more likely to be on Saturday evening. By the way, I have to issue an official warning here. You must remember to use caution at all times. It's vital the Baxters don't have a clue they're being watched; these people can be . . . highly dangerous.'

'Don't worry,' I said. 'I'm no stranger to danger.' And I pointed at all the thrillers I'd read.

'One last thing,' he said. 'On the bus I can't talk to you about any of this. But if I should need to communicate anything of a top-secret nature . . .'

'Yes?' I said eagerly.

'I daren't trust the phone or e-mail – I'll give you my numbers, but you can't use them for spy business so I shall accidentally-on-purpose bump into you. Afterwards you'll find I've left a blank piece of paper in your pocket. Would you please hold it up to a bright light? There you will see my message. Read it and memorize it, as the message will completely disappear in about two hours. And just so's you know the letter is authentic, I'll end it with the mark of my signet ring here.' He pointed to the ring on his finger. 'Look for that at the bottom of any correspondence . . . if it's not there, you'll realize immediately it isn't genuine.'

At that moment, I knew I'd breathed my last ever bit of dull air.

Chapter Eight

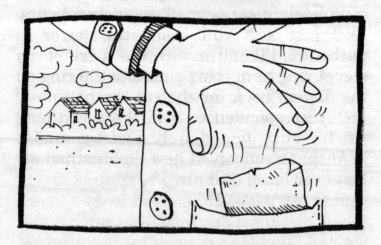

The very next morning I had my first ever live drop, and if you're not sure what a live drop is, well ... READ ON.

I'd seen Henry on the bus but I just said, 'Hello,' as I was with Eva. She's older than me and usually totally ignores me, unless she wants to boast about something. That day it was where she was going for her holidays: yawn, yawn.

Anyway, Eva and I had just got off the bus when Henry came up and proceeded to slam his heavy bag down on my foot. Under the circumstances I thought my yelp of pain was pretty restrained.

'I'm really sorry,' he murmured and moved away.

'What a loser,' cried Eva, totally unaware that a secret message – of possibly national importance – had been secreted into my left pocket. Of course, I was desperate to read it.

But Eva walked with me all the way to school, still going on about her stupid holiday. Then I dived into the loos and for once they were empty. So I yanked out that blank paper Henry had passed to me. I held it up to the light and after a few seconds brown writing started forming. Can you think of a more brilliant way to start the day?

There was just one problem – half the message was illegible. So all I could read was: *'Chief goldfinch expected to arrive . . .'* and nothing else, except for Henry's signet ring imprint at the bottom.

I was mad with frustration. I mean, I'd worked out that 'Chief goldfinch' was probably the Scorpion. But when exactly was he arriving? I guessed it was very soon, or Henry wouldn't have bothered with the live drop. But how soon? This morning? Should I speed back home now?

I had no choice but to call Henry on his mobile.

He said, 'I'm very sorry for banging that bag down on your foot. I don't know what happened there . . .'

'Oh, that's all right,' I said briskly. 'Love the invisible ink,' I added, to cheer him up.

'Lemon juice mixed with orange juice – it's sort of my own special recipe,' he added proudly.

'The only problem is, Henry – half of the message is missing.'

'You're joking.'

'No.'

'But that's terrible . . . I told you I was a very bad spy, didn't I?'

'Look, it'll be all right: I'll whisper what I've got. Then you tell me very quietly the rest.' So I said softly, *'Chief goldfinch expected to arrive* . . . And that's it.'

'Do you know, I just don't know what happened there. But the rest of the message is' – and he hissed – *'expected to arrive tonight.'*

'Tonight!?' I gasped.

'Yeah, I know – very exciting. And the message ended' – he started whispering again – *'I'll be round about half past six* . . . well, best not to say any more on the phone.'

'Right. But I can't wait to see chief goldfinch.'

'Neither can I,' said Henry. 'Bye.'

After that I went for a little walk on my own on the back field. These girls were looking at me, thinking I'd gone mad, especially as I was late for registration and got a right telling off, but I didn't care. I hardly even heard what my form teacher said. I was too busy thinking about tonight and catching up with the Scorpion.

At break time I examined that paper again. And I felt a little stab of excitement as I saw that all the words had vanished.

It was only during afternoon registration I suddenly remembered something truly terrible. I expect you have as well. That's right: I was supposed to be going out with Leo that night. We were going to the cinema. And Leo hadn't been too impressed at seeing Henry suddenly clumping down the stairs on Wednesday either, so I'd made up my mind to be extra nice to him tonight.

Oh, why couldn't the Scorpion have arrived one day later? I thought. And then I was highly ashamed of my unprofessional attitude. Catching traitors was far more important than going to the pictures with boys – yes, even fit-looking ones.

So, at the end of school I left a message on Leo's mobile, saying I was in a raging torment from a headache. I added a couple of deep groans for atmosphere. I hated doing that. But I thought, once I've helped catch these traitors I'll be able to tell Leo the truth. And he'll be so proud of his new girlfriend then.

On the way home, who should I see getting out of a taxi but Mr Baxter! I watched him go into Mrs Jenkins's local shop, which is supposed to sell absolutely everything. It had been looking very tatty, but recently it had had a bit of a face-lift. And now even posh people like Mr Baxter frequented it.

He came out of the shop a few moments later. He threw a newspaper into the bin and then he put an entire bar of chocolate into his mouth at once. Talk about greedy. And I just couldn't take my eyes off him. I kept saying to myself: So this face is what an enemy agent looks like.

Quite suddenly, his small, dark eyes

locked on to mine. And they had an odd look in them. He must have noticed me watching him.

'Hello there,' he said in his clipped tones.

'Hello . . .' I frantically searched my mind for something else to say. 'Got any plans for the weekend?' I burst out.

His eyes widened in surprise. Well, I'd never said anything other than a hello to him. Now here I was wanting to know all about his weekend.

'It depends how much hotter it gets,' he said.

'Oh yes,' I said, and then laughed merrily, for no reason in particular. He didn't join in. I was acting so suspiciously. Why, I could blow this whole operation. Then I cried out, 'By the way, how are your goldfinches getting along?'

A faint smile hovered over his thin lips. 'Another one who's interested in them, are you?'

'Oh yes, very, very interested.'

'Well, the parents are being kept very busy feeding their young, who all seem to be thriving. But my wife's the nature-lover, not me. I'll tell her you've asked about them.'

We seemed to be getting along pretty well until he said to me, quite angrily, 'And try and stay out of the sun,' before walking quickly away.

'*Try and stay out of the sun.*' What an odd thing to say. Was he showing a sudden concern for my health? Or was that a kind of coded warning? Was he really saying: '*Keep out of my business.*' But he couldn't know I was on to him – or could he?

Then I remembered that newspaper he'd hurled into the bin. Sometimes in stories a message is left in a newspaper for someone else to pick up.

So I removed the paper from the bin and examined it very carefully. I couldn't find anything until I came to the crossword on the back page. This was all filled in. Might there be a message somewhere?

Reading along one line of the crossword was GET REA. Did that mean GET READY? Now, this was a bit of a long shot; still, that paper might have been left for the Scorpion or one of his associates . . .

Back at home Dad breezed in from the garden centre. 'So what are you and Leo going to see at the pictures tonight?'

'Actually, Dad, there's been a slight change of plan. I'm not seeing Leo – now.'

'Oh dear.'

'No, it's fine, I've just shifted things around a bit and I'm doing some more goldfinch-watching again tonight – with Henry.'

'You've turned down an evening out to watch a few birds?' exclaimed Dad.

'Yes, it's becoming a massive hobby of mine.'

Dad started chewing his lip again. 'Well, all right, if that's what you want to do,' he said quietly.

'It really is.' And I grinned at him. Was he going to get a surprise later on tonight when I helped capture the Scorpion and expose the Baxters' true traitorous identity!

Later Julia called to wish me luck with my date with Leo. She wasn't very impressed when I told her I was staying in with a bad headache. 'Since when?' she demanded, in a voice reeking with suspicion.

'Since I got home, and thanks for your sympathy.'

It felt so weird lying to Julia. But as

I kept telling myself, it wouldn't be for long.

At exactly half past six the doorbell rang. I raced to answer it, and then jumped about three metres in the air.

It was Leo.

Chapter Nine

'Hi there,' I quavered.

'Just brought you these round,' Leo said, handing me some chocolates.

'Oh, you shouldn't have done that.'

'Yes I should . . . So how are you feeling?' he asked.

'Oh, I'm a bit better.' I gave what I hoped was a brave sigh. 'I've just got to be patient – and know I will be well again one day.' I was just so anxious to close the door and for him to go; if Henry turned up now, it would be a catastrophe.

But Leo went on, 'My mum gets these really bad headaches. Has to sit in her bedroom with all the curtains drawn. But she gets me to massage her shoulders and neck, and do you know, that always helps to stop them.'

'How amazing,' I murmured.

'I could come and do a massage for you, if you like.'

'Oh, I don't want to put you to all that trouble.'

'No trouble at all . . . and I know my mum would recommend me. In fact, she says I'm the best there is at getting rid of headaches.' Then he glanced at me. 'You do look a bit groggy.'

Actually, I felt incredibly groggy as I kept imagining Henry bumping into Leo.

'I really think I'd better go and lie down now,' I gasped.

'Oh, OK,' said Leo, sounding disappointed. 'Well, see you soon.'

'Oh, definitely. Bye.'

I slammed the door and heaved a great sigh of relief, until I realized I was being observed by Dad, his eyebrows rocketing.

Then the doorbell rang again.

'And here's boyfriend number two,' muttered Dad.

'He's not my boyfriend,' I hissed crossly

at him. 'He's a bird-watcher . . . and would you look after these chocolates for me? You can even eat some if you like.'

Dad took the chocolates, shaking his head.

Henry stood on the doorstep, with binoculars once again round his neck. He said quietly, 'I observed Leo approaching your house and thought it would be best to make myself scarce while he was here.'

'Well done,' I cried, before adding, 'All we're trying to do is catch some traitors . . . yet everything's getting so complicated.'

And the complications weren't over as Dad strolled over to Henry saying, 'Well, you've certainly inspired my daughter's interest in bird-watching. So how long have you been a fan of our feathered friends?' He gave this odd little chuckle, as if he'd just made a joke.

Henry replied, 'It all started when I heard this really beautiful bird song, just couldn't get it out of my head. And I had to find out which bird it was. At first I thought it was a robin, then a great tit. By the time I'd worked it out – it was a black-bird – I was well and truly hooked . . .'

Henry went on for ages like this. I mean, even I nearly believed him. As for Dad – well, he was just gripped. And at the end he said, in this low voice, 'This is all very interesting . . .'

Upstairs I told Henry he was 'brilliant', twice. He replied, 'All that extra work on my bird-watching cover has certainly paid off.'

We were both so high then, and just ready for the Scorpion to put in an appearance. We sat glued to the window, notebooks at the ready, tense, expectant . . . and not a single person went in or out of the Baxters' house that evening.

I said, 'Maybe the Scorpion will turn up in the middle of the night.'

'My bosses don't think that is very likely, as cars coming and going are bound to attract attention in a small village like this. And they don't want to do anything to arouse any curiosity.'

So it was all very disappointing. Still, as Henry said, 'You need a lot of patience in the spying game.' And he did bring me what he called 'a couple of extremely useful pieces of kit' from his bosses.

First of all, a set of headphones which

looked like an iPod, but was actually a secret listening device which you secured to your belt. 'We call it the magic ear,' he said, 'because it enables you to hear sounds a long way off.'

'I'll certainly give that a try,' I said.

Then he handed me what looked like a chunky pen, but it had a telescope fitted inside it, with a range of seven miles.

'That's our spy pen . . . everyone gets issued with one of those.'

'And now I've got one,' I said, feeling like a real insider.

'When you're fourteen and have passed loads of exams you get a second pen; that one has a cartridge of poison gas inside it, enabling you to knock out your enemies in seconds.'

'Hey, I bet you can't wait to get your hands on that.'

'No, I really can't.' Then he added: 'By the way, the spy pen I gave you has got a second use, which I'll just mention . . .'

'Mention away.'

'We carry this spy pen with us everywhere. But if ever we're in trouble, we'll try and leave it behind somewhere, as it's like our secret signal that something is very wrong. So if you ever discover an abandoned spy pen, you know someone's been abducted or is in mortal danger. Not that you'll ever need to worry about that.'

'It's useful to know all the same,' I said.

Next morning I was up before seven, keeping watch on the Baxters with my spy pen. Later on I saw Mrs Baxter watering her plants and then Mr Baxter came outside too.

I quickly slipped outside wearing my 'magic ear'. I tried to look as if I were intent on music, not eavesdropping. And at first everything went beautifully. I could hear Mr Baxter saying, 'I don't know why you're getting so worked up.'

'I'm not,' replied Mrs Baxter. 'I was merely pointing out . . .'

'No, you're panicking,' Mr Baxter replied. 'And it's not necessary, I told you Mas—'

And then I couldn't hear any more. Instead there was all this static. I shook my magic ear furiously. I caught an odd extra word of the Baxters' conversation – but no more, before all this static started up again.

Then I looked up and for just a moment I had the oddest feeling I was being watched by Mr Baxter. Then Dad called me. He was having one of his mad cleaning frenzies, making the house 'ship-shape'. He'd even drawn up a list of things we had to do.

Later that afternoon on my way back from the shops I saw Mrs Baxter. She was hanging about outside her house, as if she were watching for someone.

She was one of those people who always seemed to have their nose in the air. Rather grand and superior, except for her hair. Funnily enough, that was always very long and straggly.

Now, I'd never had one conversation with the woman, but here she was, smiling at me and saying, 'My husband tells me you're interested in our goldfinches.'

'Yeah, that's right,' I said. 'Love gold-finches – they're so colourful, aren't they?'

Her smile grew wider. 'Well, there's quite a lot of activity there now,' she said, pointing at her house, her rings flashing in the sun, 'if you'd like to have a look.'

In a kind of trance I followed her – I didn't even think to go indoors and leave

Dad a note to say where I'd gone, which was something he and Mum *always* insisted upon. And all the time I couldn't help feeling this sudden friendliness was extremely odd.

What was she up to?

Chapter Ten

She led me round the back. Mum and Dad didn't know the Baxters well – we'd been in their house once when they'd just moved in and that was about it – but I'd been invited round a couple of times by the previous owner so I'd been into the garden before. The old owner was a character all right, dead ancient, and just let his garden run excitingly wild. I remember once he invited me round to pick strawberries, which he never remembered planting. I noticed there were three new locks on the gate now. And plastic spikes on the top to stop people climbing over as well.

All sides of the garden were screened by shrubs and it was even more overgrown than I remembered it. I was admiring some of the weeds (and weeds do have their special charms, you know) when Mrs Baxter called: 'Look!' so sharply she made me jump.

Then I saw a flash of bright colours as a goldfinch flew down with a graceful swoop into the hedge.

Mrs Baxter said, 'They've been rushing about all morning – such a wonderful sight. Oh look, he's off again.' We watched the goldfinch dart away once more. Then she started firing questions at me about bird-watching. I had a strong suspicion she was testing me out. Luckily I could just repeat everything Henry had said yesterday. And that hour and a half on the internet came in dead useful too.

And finally, I saw Mr Baxter come towards us with a tray of cold drinks.

'Oh lovely,' cried Mrs Baxter. 'We've been having such a good discussion about bird-watching. It's so nice to meet a fellow enthusiast.'

Mr Baxter handed me a glass of orange juice, tinkling with ice, and said casually,

'We saw you earlier today. That was a long-range listening device you had there, wasn't it?'

I nearly spilled the drink all over myself with shock. Now what should I do? Deny it was anything of the sort?

But Mr Baxter continued, 'I recognized the make at once.'

And I replied, 'Yes, that's right. It was a present to help me catch more bird songs.'

They both smiled and nodded. But I wondered suddenly if the real reason they'd invited me round here was to let me know I'd been rumbled. They were actually giving me a warning.

Another thought came to me, which made my glass jangle even louder. Could this drink be drugged, maybe even with a truth serum? Now, in what book had that happened?

Suddenly a goldfinch came soaring back again. And while the Baxters were gazing up at it I tipped the entire contents of my glass onto the dandelions flourishing beside me.

Mrs Baxter returned her gaze to me. 'My, you were thirsty,' she said. 'Would you like another glass?'

I shook my head firmly and left shortly afterwards.

That evening I told Henry what had happened.

He said, 'I don't want to alarm you in any way . . . but I do think the Baxters wanted you to know you'd been seen. I also think they were checking out your cover story.'

'Well, it was just so lucky you said all that stuff to Dad about bird-watching yesterday. I repeated every word and I'm pretty certain they believed me.'

'Oh, so am I,' cried Henry at once. 'You've done really well . . . The one thing we don't want is for them to get suspicious – and disappear.'

'Is that likely?'

'You'd be amazed how often that happens . . . so we must be extra-vigilant. I also think it's best you don't use the magic ear again.'

'It's rubbish anyway – you hear about eight words, and then all you get is static.'

'I'll take it back to the shop,' said Henry at once.

'The shop...? I thought your bosses gave it to you.'

'Yeah, of course – what am I talking about? I'll return it to my bosses is what I meant.'

It was only a little slip, and I didn't think much about it then, especially as something really exciting happened shortly afterwards.

I was relating to Henry what I'd overheard Mr and Mrs Baxter say. 'And they were talking about someone called ... *Mas*. That's all I heard.'

Quick as a flash Henry asked, 'It couldn't have been *Massingham*, could it?' And all at once he was watching me really intently.

I thought that was a bit of a long shot actually. But because I could sense he wanted me to say 'yes' so badly, I cried, 'Yes ... yes, it just might ...' And then I started convincing myself, I suppose. 'It could very easily.' Suddenly there was a smile on his face a mile wide.

'Come on then, tell me, what's the significance of that name?' I asked.

He paused for a moment. 'This is top-secret information which you must never repeat to anyone.'

71

'Just tell me,' I cried.

Henry, still grinning wildly, said, 'Massingham is only the name the Scorpion is using. I was told that tonight. And now the Baxters are talking about him. Well, that means he's got to turn up here very soon, doesn't it?'

There was no sign of him that Saturday night though. We watched until well after nine o'clock. But we both sensed he was close by. And it really wouldn't be long now until he appeared.

I was saying goodbye to Henry at the door when he suddenly hissed, 'Look.' And there, sitting on the garden wall, was Dad chatting with . . . Leo.

I tell you, I could have died of surprise right then. What was going on?

Henry whispered to me, 'Probably better if I just go,' and stole off in about two seconds.

I went over to Leo and Dad, who seemed to be deep in conversation. Dad was saying, 'Funny how girls always had to wash their hair the night I asked them out.'

Then they both noticed me hovering and Dad shot up. 'Well, it's time an old party like me was inside . . . don't be long, Tasha.'

'No, Dad,' I murmured.

Then he patted Leo on the shoulder and said, 'Do you know, I wouldn't be a teenager again for all the tea in China,' before ambling off.

I sat down beside Leo. 'This is a surprise . . .'

'Just thought I'd call round . . .'

'And you got ambushed by my dad, I'm sorry.'

'No, I like him,' he said.

'Yeah, he grows on you. Like ivy?' I grinned, but Leo didn't smile back.

Instead he asked, 'How's your headache tonight?' with a definite note of challenge in his voice.

'Oh, the headache's over now and I'm as good as new.' But I felt so awkward and embarrassed as if Leo had just caught me out.

I think he felt he had too, because he said fiercely, 'So does that guy bird-watch in your bedroom every single night?'

'Well, there's such a lot of goldfinch activity at the moment . . . I expect things will calm down soon.'

'I think it's time he bird-watched somewhere else.'

'It's just that my bedroom has got such a great view.'

'There are other places . . .' Then he muttered under his breath, 'No one's that interested in goldfinches. I want you to tell him to sling his hook.' I could see Leo's point of view completely, only there was no way I could agree with his demand. Not with the Scorpion due any moment.

Then across the road I saw Mr Baxter come out with his watering can. Rather late to be watering his plants, wasn't it? Or was that just an excuse to see what was going on?

It was then I knew I had to do something which I was going to really hate . . . but it wasn't fair on anyone – including Leo – for things to go on like this.

'Leo,' I said quietly. 'Would you mind very much if we didn't see each other for a few days?'

Leo reeled back as if I'd just shot him. He couldn't speak for a couple of moments. Then that wounded, confused look, which had never left his face tonight, suddenly magnified. 'So you're dumping me?'

'No, of course I'm not,' I said at once.

'You're not?'

'Oh no.' I touched his arm. 'I'm dumping you very temporarily, which is a totally different thing.'

He turned away and asked through clenched teeth, 'Just tell me why you're doing this, Tasha?'

And because he looked so totally confused and lost, I burst out, 'I'm dumping you very temporarily, Leo . . . for the good of our country.'

Right away I knew I'd been highly indiscreet, especially with Mr Baxter still busily watering just a few metres away, so before Leo could reply I hissed, 'Please don't ask me any more and don't reveal to anyone what I've told you tonight.'

He gaped at me. 'But what *have* you told me?'

'One day soon you will understand, I promise.' Then I got up and whispered, 'But right now I've got a job to do, Leo, so be patient with me. Bye.'

He didn't answer but as I walked away he called after me, 'No girl's ever dumped me before.'

He still hadn't grasped the highly temporary nature of this dumping – and it was too dangerous to explain any further.

I'd already said too much. So I just gave him a cheery wave and called, 'Thanks for dropping round. See you very soon.'

Upstairs as I watched Leo stumbling away, I let out a long deep sigh; he really was very good looking. And I thought, the things I do for Britain.

Chapter Eleven

'Tell me, has your brain dropped out?'

It was the following morning and that greeting on the phone could only have come from – Julia.

She swept on. 'Because I can't think of any other explanation . . . it is true that you've dumped Leo?'

'He's been round to see you then?'

'I'm far too ugly right now for any boy to see me. He'd have nightmares for weeks. But we had a very long chat on the phone. And he's incredibly upset.'

'I know . . . but I really did try and explain it to him.'

'Well, explain it to me,' snapped Julia. 'And also tell me why you've started hanging out with the most boring boy on this planet. I mean, what in the name of lunacy is going on there?'

Now I was stuck, because I couldn't possibly tell Julia the truth. I'd said too much to Leo last night (even though I don't think he understood a word of what I'd told him), so it seemed there was only one way out of this. I'd have to pretend I really liked Henry. I'd only need to do this until the Scorpion was apprehended. And it would also be a good test of my skills at deception. If I could fool Julia, that would be very impressive.

'All right,' I said, 'the truth is, I've liked Henry in secret – for a little while, actually.'

'You never told me.'

'No. I kept it a secret, even from you. I didn't think you'd understand . . . and you don't, do you?'

Julia was actually silent for two seconds. So I went on, 'But lately my feelings for him have just bubbled over.'

'Come on, this is a joke, right?'

'It's no joke, Julia.'

'We are talking about the same person . . . that six stone of geeky pointlessness who looks like an elf and falls over his own feet every time he gets off the bus?'

'There's much more to Henry than that.'

'He's hypnotized you,' cried Julia wildly.

I laughed.

'Of course, I knew he liked you . . .'

That temporarily took my breath away. 'Did you?' I gasped.

'Oh yes, he's given you some very longing glances on the bus – and what's this about him bird-watching in your bedroom?'

'He's very interested in bird-watching.'

'While you have no interest in it at all . . . yes, I can see how much you've got in common. Plus he's got all the charisma of plankton, so you must have some great evenings together.'

'You just don't know Henry,' I said, then added completely truthfully, 'There's a very surprising side to him.'

Julia made a noise like gas escaping, and then growled: 'About your taste in boys?'

'Yes?'

'Get some,' she snapped and rang off.

But I had a horrible feeling Julia wouldn't leave it there. I was ready for another biting phone call. What I hadn't expected was for Julia to rush round to my house. Dad had just left for the garden centre (even though our garden's dripping with plants already) when Julia appeared on my doorstep.

'Feeling better?' I asked.

'No, worse.' She tottered up the stairs and then fell onto a chair in my bedroom. 'That conversation we had about Henry Grimes . . . please tell me I dreamed that.'

'Look, he's a very interesting person.'

'Then he's had a personality transplant since I last saw him.' She leaned forward. 'Come on, there's something you haven't told me about all this.'

'There isn't.'

'I know there is. So what is it?'

I got up. 'Look, Julia—' I started, and I was just casually looking across the road when a large car I didn't recognize pulled up outside the Baxters'. Then I watched a man get out. He was very big. In fact he looked a bit like a bull in a suit. The Scorpion? It could be, only he didn't have a beard. But he might very easily have shaved that off. I needed to check him out immediately with my spy pen – but I had to do this without Julia getting suspicious.

'This looks like an ordinary pen,' I said to Julia, 'but actually it's also a telescope.'

'Here, let me see,' cried Julia, getting up.

'No, wait a sec.' I was just getting the possible Scorpion into focus when Julia snatched it away.

'No you don't,' I cried and grabbed it right back from her. But by the time I'd got him in focus again he'd walked into the Baxters' house.

I gave a little groan. Then I noticed Julia looking at me oddly.

'You went mad when I took that pen,' she said.

'No I didn't,' I said. 'I just didn't like the way you snatched it from me. That was rude.'

Julia started backing away from me. 'Now I don't think it's Henry Grimes who's had the personality transplant . . . it's you.'

'Oh, don't be silly.'

'No, you are seriously weird today.'

I tried to laugh. 'Look, you can borrow the pen now.'

'I don't want it,' said Julia, sitting down again. 'I just want my friend back and not this scary look-alike who's here now.'

'I've never heard anything so silly,' I cried, while whispering to myself, 'Act naturally, act naturally.' But it's surprisingly difficult to do this when a major traitor might be directly opposite your house. And what should I do now? I had to do something.

Then I pointed to the montage of photos above my bed. 'Julia, what do you think of the new photo up there?' And as she got up and squinted at them, I scribbled the Scorpion's car numberplate onto my hand.

'There's no new picture here,' said Julia.

'Isn't there . . . ? Oh well, never mind. Look, make yourself at home. I'll be back in a sec.' Before Julia could reply I sped into the bathroom with my mobile.

I quickly tapped out Henry's number. 'Come on, answer, answer,' I cried. But then I heard a voice asking me to leave a message. Of all the times for Henry to be out! I shook with frustration before hissing, 'Henry, I think the chief goldfinch has landed. Please advise what I should do the very second you get this. Bye.'

Then I tried to stroll back into my bedroom as if I didn't have a care in the world. Julia was standing by the window looking across the road. 'He didn't stay long,' she muttered.

'Who?'

'That man you're so fascinated by, the one in the posh car.'

'What!' I yelled. 'He's going?'

'It looks like it, yes,' cried Julia. 'But what's it to you?'

'Nothing at all,' I screamed. 'Bye.'

'Where are you going?'

'I just need some fresh air.' Then I snatched my mobile and charged down the stairs. If I could get a picture of the Scorpion, that would prove he'd been here, wouldn't it? It could be vital evidence against the Baxters, in fact.

I sprinted outside. Yes, the Scorpion was still there – standing by the car, laughing away with the Baxters. He was so confident, so full of himself, he made me sick. Well, I was about to wipe that smirk off his face.

I held my mobile up to my ear as if I

were talking to someone, thinking, whatever I do, I mustn't arouse any suspicions. But all the time I was waiting for my moment to snap the Scorpion.

Now he was shaking hands with Mr Baxter. Could there be a more perfect shot? 'Got you!' I muttered triumphantly.

Then, all at once, I heard someone calling my name. It was Mrs Baxter. She'd seen me take the photograph. Now she was going to try and snatch my mobile away. She walked over towards me. I hastily shoved the mobile into my jeans pocket.

'Oh sorry, were you on the phone?' she asked.

'No, just finished. It was only one of my mates telling me about her night out.' I had to sound as normal as possible.

'Well, I just thought you'd like an update on the baby goldfinches . . .' She chatted away to me, but all the time I was aware that the Scorpion was getting into his car. Was Mrs Baxter really here just to distract me? Then, with a toot of the horn, the Scorpion was off. Mrs Baxter turned and waved to him.

Feeling a bit reckless now, I gave the Scorpion a little wave as well. He wouldn't be smiling soon.

Suddenly I noticed Mrs Baxter's face freeze. At once I realized what she'd seen: the Scorpion's car number all over my hand. She said stiffly, 'Anyway, I'd better let you get on.'

'Yes, well thanks so much for keeping me posted about the goldfinches.'

'A pleasure.' But she whipped the words at me – and her eyes seemed to grow smaller and darker.

As she walked across the road I heard someone bellow, 'Why did you just take a photo of that man?'

Julia was standing in the doorway and her question seemed to echo all the way down the road.

I sped over to her. 'Keep your voice down,' I hissed.

'Why?'

'Well, it's Sunday afternoon.'

'And the chief goldfinch has landed, hasn't he?'

I gave a shocked gasp. 'You listened outside the bathroom . . . that's unethical.'

'Not when your friend starts acting like

a five-star nutcase, it isn't. All this crazi-ness has got something to do with Henry, hasn't it?'

Her voice sounded so loud I half-pushed her inside. 'Look, I'll tell you upstairs.'

'The truth this time,' said Julia.

Chapter Twelve

No way could I tell Julia the truth. But I decided I'd give her a teeny little clue as to what was going on – just to shut her up. Of course my mind was whirling. I mean, I'd just photographed the Scorpion for goodness' sake, I was giddy with excitement. But I was also agitated that Henry hadn't rung me. Where on earth was he? So I wasn't myself at all. But I'm going on about this too much, aren't I? Well, the truth is I'm a bit ashamed of what happened next.

I started by saying, 'Henry and me—'

'Just hearing that phrase makes me shiver,' interrupted Julia.

I gave her a look. 'Henry and me are involved in a special operation, which is also very hush hush . . . but I can't say any more.'

'Why?'

'National security,' I hissed.

Julia started to laugh. This annoyed me actually. I mean, I like a joke, but I do get sick of always being the joke.

'You've finally flipped,' cried Julia.

'Yes, that's right,' I snapped. 'I knew it was a waste of air telling you anything . . . Well, I'll just say you won't be the person laughing soon.'

Julia looked at me. I think she wanted to say something else but she didn't. Instead, she gazed outside the window for a few moments before saying slowly, 'You're spying on your neighbours. And Henry has put you up to it, am I right?'

'I really couldn't say.'

'Come on, you may as well tell me the whole story. I've practically guessed it all.'

'No, you haven't.'

'You know you can trust me.'

'I can trust you to laugh.'

'I promise I won't even smile. Go on, you're bursting to tell me, really.'

She was right there. Well, I was proud of what I'd been doing. Then I told myself that as Julia had guessed some of it already . . . Yes, all right, that's no excuse, I shouldn't have said any more. But I did. 'What I tell you must not leave this room . . .' Then I stopped. 'You're laughing already.'

'No honestly. I just burped.'

Then in a low, calm voice I said, 'Well, prepare yourself for a massive shock. Henry is, in fact . . . a spy.'

'Says who?' cried Julia at once.

'No, he really is one: junior investigative operator is his full title.'

'Another would be: dirty great liar.'

'It took me a while before I believed him too,' I said. 'But think about it, the government recruits children because no one would ever suspect them of being spies. I know it sounds incredible—'

'What's incredible is that they picked Henry Grimes.'

'But don't you see,' I said. 'They choose the most unlikely people deliberately – real spies have got to be the person you least suspect.' I ended up telling Julia everything, starting with the night I saw

Henry hanging about outside my house and finally by declaring, 'I may very well have seen the Scorpion here today, and I could have the evidence that would convict the Baxters and him.'

'So this is a big moment in your life?'

'The biggest.'

For a couple of seconds I even thought Julia was with me, sharing in the drama of it all. But then she said, 'No doubt in years to come, coaches will pull up outside your house. Yes, here it is, they'll say – the very place where a twelve-year-old girl helped capture a major enemy agent. I bet there'll be a great big plaque on the wall and who knows, they might even give your house a brand new name . . . how about "The Spy Catcher"?'

'You're hilarious,' I muttered bitterly. 'You just can't believe Henry's a spy,' I said, 'because your image of spies is all from films – not real life. Well, I feel sorry for you actually.'

Julia didn't say anything for a few moments; she just stood there radiating scorn and disbelief. 'I'll tell you what I believe,' she cried at last. 'Ever since he moved into the village, I've seen Henry gazing moonily at you on the bus – you're his dream girl . . .'

I made scoffing noises.

'No, you are, but you're also way out of his league. He knows that. But he's also fascinated by you. He even stands outside your house in the hope of glimpsing you. But he writes stupid stuff down in his notebook to cover up for the fact it's you he's watching.'

I made even louder scoffing noises.

'He's so mad about you. Only nothing in the world would make you look at him . . . but then he gets run over gazing up at you. He pretended he was bird-watching. But you quickly see through that and then he makes a major discovery. You don't only like reading thrillers, you want to live right inside one. So he makes up a thriller just for you – with himself in the lead role of course, as a boy spy.'

'Now that's where you're wrong,' I cut in, 'because he didn't show off and pretend to be this amazingly brave spy . . . he tells me about all the mistakes he's made and how he only just scraped a pass in his exams.'

'But that's just to get your sympathy – which he gets in spades. Yet you're intrigued as well. A real-life spy here in Little Farthingwell.' Julia sighed. 'I can almost feel sorry for him because he knows you wouldn't want the real him who's not a spy. So he's got to keep this pretence going on as long as possible.' Then she looked right at me. 'He's lying to you, Tasha.'

I shook my head. 'No.'

'And you're making a fool of yourself.'

Stung now, I cried, 'Don't you dare say that!'

'Why not? It's true . . . A big fool. And if it gets out that a scrawny little geek made you believe he's a spy, you'll be a laughing stock all over again. Don't forget, it was only a few weeks ago you dug up that garden in the middle of the night . . .'

'Thanks for reminding me.'

'You've only just started living that down.'

I glared at her. 'Henry *is* a spy.'

Julia shook her head sadly at me. 'Tasha, he's no more a spy than I am. By the way, he got Leo nicely off the scene, didn't he? All this stuff about the Scorpion dropping in for tea at the very time you and Leo have got a date. Very clever.'

'I can't believe you're being so nasty.'

'Oh, Tasha, I'm not – but as your best friend . . .'

'It is your duty to patronize me at every opportunity.'

Julia tried to laugh. 'Oh come on, don't be a big sulk-pot.'

But not even a flicker of a smile crossed my face.

Julia swallowed and said quietly, 'You're really cross with me this time, aren't you?'

'No, I'm not cross . . . I'm ANGRY, with a capital everything.' Then I got up and said flatly, 'Bye, Julia, don't hurry back, will you?'

She got up, highly annoyed too, and marched to the door, but then she stopped. 'Just one last thing: I bet Henry will say that man you've snapped isn't the Scorpion. For if it is, then Henry hasn't any excuse to come round here again as the case is closed. You see if I'm not right.'

'No, this time you're completely wrong.'

Then I heard Julia walk quickly down the stairs. We'd had disagreements before, of course; we're so opposite you wouldn't think we could stay in the same room together for five minutes, let alone be best friends. But this was different. We were both convinced we were right, but only one of us could be. The other would be humiliated.

And then my mobile rang – and I saw that it was Henry.

Chapter Thirteen

When I told Henry what had happened he was round my house faster than the speed of light. And I was just buzzing with excitement. I don't think I've ever felt so alive.

I waited breathlessly for him to say what a brilliant job I'd done snapping the Scorpion. And he sort of did. He said my photograph would have been vital evidence if he had been the Scorpion. Only it wasn't. He could see how I thought it was, but the real Scorpion had still got the white beard and was taller and with a much fatter face.

Henry brought round a picture of the real Scorpion that night – which he said I could keep, so I wouldn't get mistaken again. He said he'd been given this photo at a de-briefing with his 'spy mum' this afternoon. And it showed the Scorpion sitting at a table, chuckling away with another man. Oddly enough, the other man looked familiar and I wondered if I could have seen him around recently. But Henry said, rather crisply I thought, that was impossible as the other man was now in prison.

So I studied this snap of the real Scorpion very carefully. And to be honest, he didn't look especially scary. He was just a big, burly man having a joke with his mate. Of course this could all be part of his very clever disguise. Or maybe Henry had swiped this photograph from a family album, to string me along a bit longer. Yeah, the suspicions were moving in big time now. I kept remembering things like the time he'd said he'd take the magic ear back to the shop. Was that little slip a clue he was lying?

And what if . . .? But I pushed that thought right away. It was too terrible.

Only it kept coming back. And the thought was: what if Julia was right? What if Henry was only pretending to be a spy to impress me?

My head was swarming with doubts now. In fact, I got so desperate I did a little test on Henry that detectives often use. Perhaps you haven't heard of the blink test. Well, it's dead simple: you ask someone a few questions, but all the time you keep checking their blinking rate. You see, when people are lying, their eyes hardly ever blink.

So I asked Henry some stuff about spying. Couldn't tell you his answers, I was too busy watching his eyes.

He didn't blink once.

Things were looking bad for him. And then something mind-blowingly awful happened. Henry suddenly leaned forward and gave my hand a little squeeze while smiling at me in a highly alarming way. He must have spotted me staring into his unblinking eyes . . . and decided I was getting all swoony about him.

I gaped at him through a thick fog of horror. Could Julia be right? Did he like me?

'Working with you on this operation has been grand,' he went on, while still beaming away at me.

Now my insides turned to ice. For no cool person would ever say 'grand', let alone a spy.

My night was totally smashed to pieces now. And I just wanted Henry to go so I could think all this out. I held my hankie up to my nose and said I sensed that a nosebleed was on its way. I made it sound like an earthquake. Henry looked worried and offered to stay and look after me. But I said Dad was around for emergencies . . . and my nosebleeds didn't usually last too long.

Anyway, I'd just seen Henry off when I suddenly noticed Dad and Leo sitting on the wall together again. Poor Leo, I thought, he just can't stay away from me. I decided I'd be a bit friendlier to him tonight.

Dad was gibbering away, but Leo was listening to him with such interest and I'm pretty certain he wasn't just being polite either. It was as if Dad were his coach or something. Then when they saw me it was Leo – not Dad, this time – who sprang up.

And Leo looked at me as if I'd just dribbled down my chin or something. It was horrible seeing such deep disgust in those gorgeous eyes of his. 'Don't worry, Tasha, your dad's explained everything and I shan't bother you again . . . unless it's to have another chat with your dad.'

A grin quickly stole across Leo's face when he said this. Dad was smiling away too. But when he said goodbye to me, Leo's face was about as warm and friendly as Count Dracula's.

After he'd cycled off I said, 'Dad, what's going on?'

'The lad came round here all mixed up and wanting to see you,' said Dad, 'and I took pity on him. It's not easy when a girl doesn't want to know, as I know.'

'But I do want to know him,' I cried.

'He told me you'd dumped him.'

'Only temporarily.'

Dad smiled in an annoyingly knowing way. 'But you like the other lad: the bird-watcher. And that's all right — you're allowed.'

'No, Dad, he's just a friend.'

Dad's smile became even more annoying if that was possible. 'Come on, tell the truth: I've seen the way your eyes light up when this Henry calls.'

'But that's only because he's a . . .'

'Yes?' asked Dad.

I turned away. 'You wouldn't understand,' I muttered. Then I had a hideous thought. 'Dad, you didn't tell Leo about my eyes lighting up when Henry called?'

'Let's say, I gave him the advice I wish I'd had at his age.' Then he rubbed his hands together. 'I'll make us a little supper now, shall I?' And he strolled inside whistling, dead pleased with himself.

I was too stunned by the cruelty of life to know what to do at first. Then I decided I had to ring Leo . . . to tell him what exactly? *I was only hanging about with Henry because I thought he was a spy. But now I'm not so sure, so I'll go out with you again?*

Anyway Leo had cycled off tonight in such a proud 'I'm-totally-over-you sort of way', thanks of course to my dad's wonderful coaching.

I tell you, it's bad enough when you're mad at other people, but it's so much worse when you're mad with yourself. Why on earth did I believe Henry so easily? I mean, it's a really incredible tale.

But he just shows me one grubby ID card and I swallow everything he tells me.

The trouble was, I wanted his story to be true so badly, I didn't bother checking it carefully enough. Sherlock Holmes would not be proud of me. And now all my hopes and dreams were just fizzling out like a wet firework. Or were they? After all, there was still no knock-out proof that Henry was lying. It might still be true.

If only there was some way I could find out for certain . . . I paced around my room, thinking and thinking.

Then I noticed the Baxters driving back. They'd been out for a couple of hours. I wondered where they'd been. Off to see the Scorpion?

The Scorpion – how much longer did I have to wait for him to turn up? That's if he even existed. And then, quite suddenly, an idea jumped into my head. It was so bold, so daring, it actually made me gasp. It was also totally crazy . . . and possibly very dangerous as well. But afterwards, well, I'd know for certain whether Henry really was a spy. And I just couldn't stand another second of all this uncertainty.

I had to do it.

Chapter Fourteen

Now I did realize I was performing a highly reckless act.

That's why I left a card in my bedroom, on which I'd written in big letters: GONE TO THE BAXTERS'. This was just in case I should mysteriously disappear. As Henry had said: 'The first rule of being a spy is that you can't be too careful.'

Oh yeah, I was still listening to him, still convinced that somehow he'd turn out to be genuine.

Then I walked out of my door and over to the Baxters' house. It was a very white-looking house . . . and tonight it seemed to shimmer at me in a ghostly sort of way. I knocked on the door. Mr Baxter opened it immediately.

He wasn't friendly or hostile. His face was blank. 'Good evening,' he said in his clipped, sharp voice. All at once Mrs Baxter was beside him. She can move dead quietly when she wants to, I thought. (Was she taught this when she became an enemy agent?) Then she gave me a wintry little smile – she was certainly not as welcoming as before – and said, 'I'm afraid all the goldfinches have retired for the night.'

'Oh, that's all right,' I said. 'I've come about something else entirely.' I could see their eyes, all serious and watching me. My heart was pounding away – not because I was nervous; I was surprisingly calm actually – but I so wanted Henry's story to be true. And in the next few seconds I'd know the truth. 'Just to let you know,' I said, 'when you were out, someone was here looking for you.'

'For us?' Mrs Baxter looked surprised while Mr Baxter's lips were pursed up as if he were about to start whistling. Interesting reactions, I thought.

'He was a very big man,' I continued, 'huge in fact, with a white beard and his name was . . . Oh, what was it? He told me not to forget it. Oh yes, he was called . . . Mr Massingham.'

So there it was. I'd done it. I felt as if I'd just sent a rocket hurtling into space. I was sure nothing would ever be the same again now.

Then I kept my eyes fixed on the two enemy agents. Now, it would have been utterly fantastic to tell you that Mr Baxter reeled backwards gasping, or Mrs Baxter was so terror-struck she started frothing at the mouth. Very sadly, that didn't happen and, to be honest, I wasn't really expecting it. These were trained spies, for goodness' sake. But I hadn't read two hundred thrillers for nothing. I knew I had to be alert for their tiniest reaction.

So, did Mr Baxter's hands give a little tremble? Or did Mrs Baxter let out a guilty gulp?

I stood there, wishing so hard for something, anything. But NOTHING, except a look of deep puzzlement and Mrs Baxter declaring, 'I'm sure we don't know anyone of that name.'

'And it's certainly one I'd remember,' said Mr Baxter. 'Massingham.' He seemed to be tasting the word. Then he shrugged his narrow shoulders.

But I wasn't ready to give up. 'That's so odd, because this Mr Massingham' – and I paused for a second after I repeated the name – 'was extremely keen to see you. In fact, he said to tell you he'd call round later.'

'When, no doubt,' said Mr Baxter easily, 'we'll know what it was all about.'

I glared at him. How dare he look so carefree!

Mrs Baxter did seem a little more concerned. 'I just wonder what this man wanted to see us about.'

'It sounded highly urgent,' I persisted.

'He probably wants to sell us something,' said Mr Baxter.

'No, I don't think so,' I cried. 'And surely not on a Sunday.'

'Oh yes, people are always trying to sell me something these days . . . they can be highly insistent as well,' said Mr Baxter. 'You wouldn't believe all the junk mail I receive; personally written to me as well . . . it's a disgrace.'

Now he sounded like my dad when he'd got the grumps.

But there wasn't a glimmer of guilt or concern on his face. And both he and Mrs Baxter's blink rates – which I'd been scrutinizing most carefully – remained steady too.

And then their grandfather clock chimed in the hallway, as if to confirm the Baxters' total respectability. Listening to it somehow seemed to bring me to my senses. I knew I couldn't spin this conversation out a moment longer.

Mr Baxter thanked me for calling round and said he'd let me know when the mystery was solved. He was still muttering about pushy salesmen as he closed the door.

And afterwards, the disappointment was like a wave hitting me. It took my breath away for a few seconds. I stood there, gasping for breath.

Then I slouched home.

Chapter Fifteen

Next morning I woke up very early. It was that time when everything's perfectly still, which normally I like, but today I just lay in bed fuming at my stupidity. How could I have fallen for Henry's tale? Anyone would think my favourite hobby was making daft mistakes. What was the matter with me?

And then, quite suddenly, I shook myself and thought, I'm sick of lying here feeling sorry for myself. It's time I did something. How about a live drop, just for Henry? I'll send him such a nice little message! I slipped downstairs, found some lemon

juice and orange juice and, with just a few
birds chirping sleepily for company, wrote:

Dear Henry
THE GOLDFINCHES HAVE ALL GONE. THEY WANTED TO
GET SOME SAND ON THEIR BEAKS, SO NOW THEY'RE
LYING ON A BEACH IN SPAIN – WITH THE KING OF BAD
BREATH, MR MASSINGHAM.
I CAN'T SAY IT'S BEEN GREAT KNOWING YOU, HENRY,
BECAUSE IT REALLY HASN'T. IN FACT, YOU ARE THE
MOST COMPLETELY LOATHSOME PERSON I'VE EVER
MET.
Tasha.

Later that morning though, on the bus
to school, there wasn't just one live drop
going off – oh no, there were two. For, just
as I was bumping into Henry and deposit-
ing my note into his left pocket, he was
also slipping a message into my right
pocket. It said:

W NO BELIEV SCORPION WILL CAL
TONIGHT WILL C ROU AT USUA TIM.

First of all, for a so-called spy, it was
pathetic that he couldn't even send a secret
message properly. But secondly, he really

thought he'd snare me again by promising the Scorpion. That news was supposed to send me mad with joy, I suppose.

A few minutes later my mobile started ringing. It was Henry, clearly totally mystified by my message. Well, let him stay mystified, I thought, as I switched my mobile off.

I ignored messages from Julia too. Sometimes you just want to be alone with your pain, don't you? But when I got off the bus home to Little Farthingwell later that afternoon, there she was, waiting for me.

'You haven't answered any of my calls, so I thought I'd better just check you hadn't been assassinated by enemy agents.'

Then she started laughing – and I joined in.

'So how are the enemy agents today, or should I say, chief goldfinch?'

'Call them what you like,' I said, 'but they've turned into dull, boring neighbours again.'

'And what about Henry?'

'These are three words I really hate saying, so there will never be a repeat performance of them . . . You were right.'

To my great surprise Julia leaned forward and gave my arm a friendly pat.

'Oh, don't be nice to me,' I cried. 'The shock might kill me.'

'Yeah, sorry about that. I don't know what came over me,' said Julia. 'The truth is, you only have to hear the word "spy" for your brain to drop out.'

'Well, it's dropped back in again now.'

'I'm very glad to hear it. So now you can concentrate on important things . . . like Leo.'

'Oh, he's totally over me . . . thanks to my dad.'

'I saw him last night, and I can assure you, he's not,' said Julia. 'By the way, did you know it's his birthday today?'

'No.'

'Well, you do now. The question is, are you going to do anything about it?'

'You mean, wish him a happy birthday?'

'This girl's a genius . . . yes, and then say your country has allowed you to go back out with him.'

We both started laughing again. Julia said she'd be back at school in a few days. 'Until then . . . don't talk to any more spies, will you?'

'You're never going to let me forget this, are you?' I cried.

'Never,' agreed Julia cheerfully.

Back at home I switched my mobile on again. Less than a minute later Henry rang me from his house: 'Oh great, you've had your mobile switched off all day, you know.'

'Oh have I?' I said vaguely, as if that was nothing to do with me.

'I got your secret message – excellent use of lemon and orange juice, by the way.'

'Thanks.'

'No, it showed real flair. You'll have to give me some tips . . . now, about what you wrote . . .'

'Which part?' I asked sweetly.

'Well, all of it really, I suppose, but especially that bit about being so loathsome. That confused me actually. Was there any special reason for you writing that?'

'Well, do you know, there was. The main one being that you're a total and complete liar.'

'Now wait a minute here.'

'Just answer me this,' I interrupted, my anger boiling up suddenly. 'Are you a spy?'

'You know I am.'

111

'Well, prove it then. You've told me you're living with a real spy, not your mum. So, if you're at home now, put that woman on the phone – the one who's pretending to be your mum.'

He sounded shocked. 'I can't do that.'

'Why not?'

'Well, what do you want to ask her?'

'About Operation Scorpion for starters.'

'But she won't tell you a thing,' he cried. 'She believes I've told you far too much already. I got an official reprimand, actually. And they made me go on a special course yesterday evening called: *How to Control Your Contacts*.'

'Shame it wasn't how to control your lying,' I snapped.

'Look, something's obviously disturbed you. How about if I nip round?'

'*Nip round.*' How could I ever have believed that a boy who said un-cool things like that could be a spy?

'You've nipped round to my house for the very last time. I never want to see you again.'

'Oh . . .' His voice fell away for a moment. 'But what about the Scorpion? We still haven't seen him.'

'And would you like to know why? Because he doesn't exist.' Tears sprang to my eyes as I said this. That's why I rang off at that point. And then I heard Dad calling me.

I ran into the kitchen, where Dad flung a carton of milk at me. 'Can you open that, because I can't?'

After a bit of a struggle I managed it.

'It's ridiculous,' said Dad in full rant now. 'Why is everything so hard to open these days? Don't they think we have enough to do with our time? Why have they got to make everything so blooming difficult?' He has a big moan about modern life once a week. Today, though, I found myself joining in.

I said, 'And have you ever tried undoing bottles of squash? They're so tight it takes about two days.'

'I know, it's crackers,' agreed Dad. 'And why are the instructions for everything these days in such small writing?'

'Or hidden away,' I added.

Dad and I moaned on like this for another twenty minutes. It was just about the best conversation he and I had ever had. It was only when I went back upstairs that I realized the terrible thing that had started happening: my deep disappointment with life was turning me into a fifty-year-old. I'll start frequenting garden centres and watching *The Antiques Roadshow* next.

Such a horrible shock made me determined to get a grip on myself. There were worse disappointments than discovering your neighbours weren't spies. I just couldn't think of any right then.

But I decided it was time to get on with my life. And I'd start by wishing Leo a happy birthday, as Julia had suggested.

Before that, though, I had a symbolic act to perform. I took one last look at my 'spy pen'. Of course it wasn't that really. Henry had probably just got it off the internet. He did go to an awful lot of trouble to impress me, didn't he?

And if he had pretended to be an actor or a footballer I could have smiled and forgiven him; but not a spy. That was just playing with my dreams.

I threw the spy pen into the bottom of one of my cupboards. Also banished there was my photograph of the Scorpion or whoever he really was. I glanced at it one last time. That man who was with the Scorpion did look awfully familiar. I was sure I'd seen him somewhere. Still, what did it matter now?

I was about to close the drawer when I suddenly added one last thing: my notebook. I decided it was a bad influence on me.

Now I really felt as if I'd come to the end of a chapter in my life. Even the weather was changing. After days and days of sunshine beaming down, low, heavy clouds were now brooding over everything. I was glad. I wanted every single thing to be different . . . even the weather.

Then I set off to see Leo, so full of good intentions.

But I never got there.

Chapter Sixteen

Leo lived right at the other end of the village, not far from Henry actually. On the way to Leo's house I passed the common. I decided I'd go for a little walk around while I worked out what I was going to say to him.

But actually, I was just putting it off. I mean, it was dead obvious what I was going to say. Two words: HAPPY BIRTHDAY.

And as I went roaming about on the common I got so mad with myself again. Either go and see Leo now or take yourself back home, I decided.

Strangely enough, not a single person was about on the common that night. Normally you see people letting their dogs off the lead or a gang of boys playing football. But tonight I seemed to have the whole common to myself.

All at once I noticed how grey and dark it had got . . . and there was that tense, expectant hush you get just before a major storm's about to break out. Usually I really like that and the way the air seems to vibrate with danger. But tonight I felt uneasy, exposed. For here I was, totally on my own, in the middle of a great wide space, with a storm revving up. Now, how daft is that?

And then out of nowhere a voice rang out, 'Natasha!' Funny, that's never felt like my name. And if you called me that I don't know if I'd even turn round. I'd assume you meant someone else.

No mistake tonight, though. Someone was calling me all right. I peered around. There seemed to be shadows all over the common now. But I couldn't make out any human figures. Of course this was where my spy pen would have been so useful – and it was really quite eerie knowing that someone was here calling my name, yet not wanting me to see them.

Then that voice – I'd already come to hate it after just one word – started up again.

'*Stay out of things that don't concern you,*' it said. I didn't recognize it at all. Still, it was probably disguised. And it sounded as if these words were being spoken through a loudspeaker, as there was a little crackle at the end of the sentence and the words seemed to echo all around me.

'*Listen to this warning or you will be very sorry,*' the voice went on. And those last two words – 'very sorry' – were carried away on a sudden gust of wind and seemed to race round and round the common.

'So is that it?' I cried out as defiantly as I could manage. 'Is the show over now?'

Not a leaf stirred. The whole common ached with silence.

That deep quiet was nearly as scary as that disembodied voice. And I tell you, my knees were knocking a bit now. But I didn't move. I suppose I was just transfixed with shock.

118

And had that person shouting a warning to me scarpered away now? Or was he or she still hidden in the shadows somewhere?

'Where are you?' I cried again, not really expecting a reply. But this time I got one all right: a sudden glare of lightning, followed almost immediately by a great roll of thunder bursting right over my head.

I started to run. Rain was tippling down now and I could hardly see where I was going. Once I stumbled and fell over. I wanted to scream and yell then, but I didn't, because it's just not something private investigators ever do. So instead, I hauled myself up and ran all the way home (I figured I couldn't turn up at Leo's looking like a drowned rat). Finally, soaking and gasping, I was back. I thudded upstairs. Luckily, Dad was still out as I really didn't want him fussing about now.

So I just gave my hair a quick rub with a towel and then sat staring out at the rain, flooded with happiness. I bet those three last words gave you a start.

But you see, halfway home I realized

something absolutely wonderful. On the common, I'd been warned off, hadn't I? Well, the only suspects (they could very easily have disguised their voices) were Mr and Mrs Baxter. That proves they did know the name 'Massingham', despite their performance on the doorstep when I questioned them. What superb actors they must be. But they really were – oh, isn't life brilliant – enemy agents.

And with rainwater still dripping down my neck I called Henry.

He sounded rather surprised to hear from me. Well, it was less than two hours ago I'd told him I never wanted to see him again. But when I said I needed him to come round urgently, he didn't hesitate. And the rain was drumming down even more heavily when he rang the doorbell.

We sped upstairs, where I told him about the eerie voice on the common. He was so concerned, he asked me three times if I was absolutely certain I was all right. He also gave my hand a little squeeze, which wasn't corny or embarrassing as you might have expected. It just felt oddly comforting actually.

And I suddenly said, 'My hair must look terrible.'

'It should do,' he said, 'but somehow it doesn't.'

Then Henry said with a highly puzzled frown, 'I'm positive it was the Baxters warning you off. But they've totally blown their cover now. It just doesn't make any sense.'

'Well, I can think of one tiny explanation,' I said shyly. 'You see, I went round to see them yesterday.'

Henry sat up with such a jump his glasses fell off. I'd never seen anyone look so shocked. My throat felt very dry.

'Yes, well the thing is, Henry – now don't get mad, well you can if you like.' My words were falling over themselves. 'I wanted to check out what you'd told me. So I pretended someone was looking for them called' – I just whispered the last two words – 'Mr Massingham.'

Henry didn't say anything, just threw out his hands in a disbelieving way.

I rushed on. 'You see, I just wanted to see their reaction when I mentioned Mr Massingham's name. And the weird thing is, they didn't seem to know the name at all. Their blink rate stayed remarkably steady too.'

'They're very skilled at deceiving people,' said Henry in a low, flat voice. 'If they weren't they'd be finished.'

'Yes, I know, and I can't believe I did something so totally stupid, can you?' My stomach felt all fluttery now, as though I was going to be sick. 'I'm just worried – well, I haven't sabotaged the whole operation, have I?'

Henry didn't answer. Instead he got up, the binoculars slung round his neck as usual, and looked across the road. And the air seemed to hum with danger again, just as it had done out on the common before the thunderstorm broke. To be honest, I felt even more scared now.

'I'm afraid you might have,' he said at last. I let out a groan of horror.

'That's the last thing I wanted,' I cried at last. 'You know that.'

Henry gave a deep, explosive sigh. 'So why couldn't you have trusted me?' he burst out.

'I'm truly sorry, but I'll do anything to put this right, Henry. Anything at all. I don't care how dangerous.'

Recovering somewhat, Henry said, 'I really think it's best you're off this case now.'

'Oh no,' I cried.

'In fact, I'm certain my boss would insist. Of course, I could be chucked out on my ear too, for believing in you.'

'Oh no,' I cried again. 'That must not happen. This is all my mess, not yours.'

'That's for them to decide,' he said quietly.

'But my bedroom's such a great look-out point. Surely they won't want to lose that,' I cried.

'There may not be anything to see now.'

'I've totally, totally messed up, haven't I?'

Henry didn't answer, he only said, 'Thanks anyway for all your help – and hospitality.'

Just as he was leaving, Dad blew in noisily, throwing his wet umbrella down. He seemed to be in a really good mood. Or maybe it was just that Henry and I were in such a gloomy one.

'So how are the goldfinches tonight?' asked Dad.

Henry looked away and I said, 'We

think they've all gone.'

'What!' exclaimed Dad.

'Yes, all flown away,' I went on. 'Someone frightened them,' I said, and added, under my breath, 'Me.'

'But that's extraordinary,' cried Dad.

'Yes, I was pretty amazed when I heard,' snapped Henry, before stalking off into the rain without another word.

'He seems upset,' said Dad.

'Can't think why,' I cried. 'They were only goldfinches.' And then tears started streaming down my face.

'Now, this isn't just about goldfinches, is it?' said Dad.

I agreed it wasn't, but of course I couldn't tell him any more. And he didn't press me. Now and again he can be surprisingly wise.

Instead he said, 'You know what you need, some of my mushroom risotto.' This has become quite a regular occurrence while Mum has been away: Dad and I having 'a little light supper' as he calls it. And I thought, well, if I go upstairs, I'll only have to listen to that voice in my head saying over and over, 'You've really blown it this time.' So instead I sat downstairs eating every morsel of Dad's mushroom risotto and having two helpings of his fruit pie afterwards.

I tell you, there's nothing like misery for giving you an appetite.

Chapter Seventeen

Next morning felt more like autumn: bleak and cold and very gloomy; it matched my mood perfectly. It felt odd putting my coat back on again. I dragged myself to the bus stop. I was shattered already – then I was suddenly aware of a grey Volvo driving slowly past me. I clocked it because the windows were all dark, so you couldn't see inside.

Maybe a reclusive rock star or a world-famous actor was reclining behind those mysterious windows. But then I figured, no, they'd be in a much swankier car than that.

Then, on the way home, I saw that grey Volvo again. I just felt a flicker of surprise at first. But all at once my private investigator's intuition took over, and I had a feeling the car with the windows you couldn't see into was keeping an eye on me.

Of course I hadn't a clue who was in the car. It could be enemy agent pals of the Baxters. It might even be the Scorpion. Or I suppose it just might be Henry's bosses trailing the girl who'd wrecked their whole operation.

I felt goosebumps running all over my skin, even after the grey Volvo had disappeared. For I knew it wasn't far away and if I went for a walk this evening it would roll slowly past me again.

To calm myself down I went into Mrs Jenkins's shop to buy some chocolate. It was empty, save for Mrs Jenkins. She was small and plump and came rolling towards you like a rubber ball. But today I thought she gave me a quick, wary look when I first entered. Then I decided I'd imagined it, but as I was leaving she called me back. 'You dropped this, dear.' She came up waving a leaflet.

'Did I?' I said in surprise.

Her hand was covering half of it and all I could see were the first three words which yelled out at me: BE VERY CARE-FUL. Then she thrust the leaflet into my hand. It was about a spot where there'd been a number of accidents recently. And I'd never seen it in my life before. Why on earth did Mrs Jenkins think it belonged to me?

Then, on the way home, a throb of terror raced through me as I wondered: had I just received my second warning? Did Mrs Jenkins know all along I hadn't dropped that leaflet? Instead she'd kept it there so that when I came in she could pounce on me with it. Funny how, at first, she'd only let me see the first three words: BE VERY CAREFUL.

Did that mean Mrs Jenkins was in league with the Baxters?

This village was turning into a hotbed of traitors.

I was still thinking about this when Julia rang. 'I thought you were going to wish Leo a happy birthday?' she demanded.

'Oh, I really was,' I said, 'until something highly significant happened.'

'You know,' said Julia, 'I met someone yesterday who looked a lot like you and she told me she had finished for ever with super-spy Henry Grimes.'

'I had,' I said, 'only something happened yesterday which totally confirmed his story.'

'I can't bear to hear this,' cried Julia, 'but I know I'll have to . . . What's Looney Tunes told you now?'

'Now even you are going to change your mind,' I said.

So I told her everything that had happened on the common, and do you know what she said – with pity in her voice? 'Oh, honestly, Tasha, you just imagined it.'

'I so did not.'

'Oh, come on, you've got an overactive imagination anyway . . . and it was dark and late . . .'

'If you say I've imagined it one more time I'm putting this phone down.' I was really mad. Sometimes Julia goes too far and treats me as if I'm about three.

'Well, all right,' said Julia. 'It was Henry disguising his voice and talking through a loudspeaker.'

'Why on earth should he do that?'

'Well, he's got you believing him again, hasn't he?'

'But he's really mad at me.'

'Oh, I think he'll be round soon, saying how his bosses have forgiven you – and you'll both be watching goldfinches before you know it.'

'Well, that isn't all,' I said. Then I told Julia about the grey Volvo following me.

'You see a car twice in one day and you immediately think you're being followed.'

'Did I mention Mrs Jenkins's warning as well?' and I told her about that.

'This is just incredible,' said Julia. 'You're seeing conspiracies everywhere. When Henry pretended to be a spy . . . well, he just didn't know what he was starting.'

'All right, I'm not absolutely definite Mrs Jenkins was warning me off. That's just a possibility. But I know for certain that I'm being followed.'

'No one is following you,' cried Julia equally firmly, 'except perhaps a man in a white coat.'

Have you ever noticed how sometimes it's your best friend who can annoy you more than anyone else in the world? Well, this was one of those occasions. I could have cheerfully throttled her at that moment. And then an idea jumped into my head.

'All right,' I said. 'I've got a little challenge for you – if you're up to it.'

'So what is it?'

'Come round and I'll tell you.' Then I added, 'It's best if you slip round to the back of my house. I want your arrival to be as inconspicuous as possible.'

'What are you up to?' she asked.

'You'll find out,' I replied mysteriously.

Well, Julia arrived at my back door a few minutes later, grumbling at having to go out on such a dark, depressing night. But, as I explained, this was perfect weather for the little deception I wanted her to take part in.

Twenty minutes later Julia left my house again, wearing one of my dresses and in my distinctive coat and hat. She'd even managed to squeeze herself into a pair of my high boots.

I also made her spend a few minutes practising my walk. Julia said she just had to make some quick, darting

131

movements, like an over-enthusiastic puppy, and she had my walk exactly.

Then I told her I was certain she would see a grey Volvo creep past her on her way home. When this happened she had to ring me and grovel for many hours.

'You'll be the one doing the grovelling,' laughed Julia.

I did feel it was my duty to warn her to be very careful. I even dug out the photograph of the Scorpion that Henry had given me.

'Look and remember,' I said gravely. And just because I was really concerned about her safety I slipped my spy pen into the palm of her hand. 'If something bad should happen, drop this spy pen somewhere where I'll find it. Then I'll know you need help.'

At this point Julia just dissolved into loud laughter. 'It must be such fun living in your world,' she gasped, 'with intrigue and excitement waiting round every corner ... it's such a shame none of it is real.'

'You're about to get the shock of your life ... ring me if you need any help.'

'Oh, behave,' laughed Julia. 'Anyway, I can't call you till I get home as I've left my mobile there – I'm out of credit. You'll just have to wait.' She was still giggling as she set off.

I must have walked round my bedroom two hundred times. I was so impatient for Julia to call me and tell me she'd seen that grey Volvo.

I waited and waited for the phone to ring . . . but then the doorbell did. It was Leo.

I was shocked and thrilled at the same time. He's found out he can't live without me, I thought. Well, I'm not surprised. It's just a shame he's called now when I'm so busy.

'Hey, Tasha,' Leo cried. 'How are you doing?'

'Oh I'm fine. You?'

'I'm safe,' he grinned. 'Just came round to say hello and . . . we are still mates, aren't we?'

'Of course we are,' I said at once.

'That's good to know, because the thing is – well, I've met up with Julia a lot lately, mainly talking about you actually.'

'Now I feel terrible,' I grinned.

'No, it's just I've never gone out with a girl like you before.'

'I should carry a government health warning, shouldn't I?'

'No, because a really good thing has happened: I've met up with Julia so many times that . . . well, the thing is . . . she's not with you, is she?'

'No.'

'Good, because I wanted to check with you first.'

'Check what?'

'Well, that you are cool about me asking her out.'

Now, I hadn't seen that coming at all. But I said shakily: 'Oh, totally cool. I'm dead happy for you both.' And I suppose I was. I was a bit miserable for myself though. I also couldn't help thinking it hadn't taken him very long to get over me: a quick chat with my dad one night and he's off after his next girlfriend.

Leo was sighing with relief. 'I just didn't want there to be any bad feelings – I hate all that kind of stuff . . . you won't mention this conversation to Julia, will you?'

'Of course I won't.'

'Because she might turn me down.' He grinned, suddenly bashful. 'You don't happen to know where she is, do you?'

At that moment a car pulled into the Baxters' drive: a grey Volvo. I watched with a kind of horrified fascination as the car went right inside the garage, just as if there was someone in that car they didn't want anyone else to see.

Then I heard Leo ask again, very politely, 'Do you know where Julia is?'

I had a horrible feeling I did. But I just mumbled, 'No, not exactly.'

Then he smiled at me in a concerned sort of way. 'You *are* all right about this, Tasha?'

'Oh, yes, couldn't be happier,' I cried, trying to tear my mind away from images of Julia being kidnapped. 'But I've got to go now. Bye.'

I closed the door and hurtled upstairs. I watched the Baxters' house intently, but no sign of any activity at all. Of course I didn't know for certain Julia had been inside that grey Volvo. She should have got home by now. So why hadn't she called me? I couldn't call her parents – Julia had told me they were out till later – and I couldn't call Henry, not while he was so angry with me. What *could* I do? Something didn't feel right about this.

And it was up to me to do *something*.

I decided I'd re-trace Julia's steps. It was only drizzling with rain now but it was dark already. But I'd remembered my torch and I shone it on every corner of the ground as I followed the exact route Julia would have taken.

Then just as I reached the bus stop, I tingled all over with shock.

For there, beneath all the bus time-tables, lay one spy pen.

Chapter Eighteen

MY CONFUSED DAD!

For just a moment my brain froze. I couldn't believe it.

I'd told Julia spies only left this pen behind if something bad had happened to them. And now here it was. Of course she might have dropped it as a joke. But right then, I knew she hadn't done that. No, this was Julia's cry for help.

She must have seen the grey Volvo. Only this time it had stopped and out had got . . . could it have been the Scorpion? I was sure it was.

He'd overpowered Julia, of course, and all she could do was drop this one, very significant clue. Now she was probably drugged and locked up.

But what a shock for the Baxters when they realized the Scorpion had brought back the wrong girl. And why did they suddenly decide to kidnap me? Was I just proving too troublesome? Or maybe they had something big planned for tonight and wanted me out of the way?

Terror was tingling in every vein of my body now. But what should I do? Well, I'd got Julia into this mess, so it was my duty to rescue her, immediately.

I rushed back and stood outside the Baxters' house. I wanted to stride in there and demand they release Julia now. But they'd just deny everything. No, I needed some back-up.

And then I saw Dad's car in our driveway. He was back from his 'big shop'.

Dad. I wouldn't normally tell him anything as important as this, but if he was standing beside me, Mr and Mrs Baxter wouldn't be able to slam the door in our faces. They'd have to let Dad inside. Then while he was talking, I could try and slip away and search for Julia. They'd have discovered they'd got the wrong girl by now, but I guess it would be just too risky to let her go.

So Julia was locked away in that house somewhere. And it was up to me to get her out.

My heart beating like a million hammers, I marched into the kitchen. Dad was filling up the freezer in the kitchen and whistling away when he saw me. 'Thought I'd start painting the kitchen ceiling tonight. Had a good day, love?' He seemed so cheerful. What a shock he was about to get – especially as he was nowhere near as knowledgeable about enemy agents as me.

'The thing is, Dad, I've got something to tell you.'

'Fire away,' he said, still piling stuff into the freezer.

'It's very important actually.'

He whirled round. 'Ah, do you want to sit down next door then?'

'Oh no, here's fine. It's just, you know you thought Henry and I were upstairs watching goldfinches. Well, actually, we haven't been doing anything of the sort.'

Dad reached forward for the side of the table, as if to steady himself. 'And what have you been doing?' he quavered.

'Watching Mr and Mrs Baxter.'

Relief shot across Dad's face, followed by a highly puzzled frown. 'But why on earth were you doing that?'

'Because they're enemy agents, Dad. I know this, as Henry is a spy – for our side. He's got proof as well: a membership card in the heel of his shoe.'

Dad stared at me, open-mouthed.

'The government recruits children because no one ever suspects them. It's very clever really, isn't it?'

Dad just went on gaping at me.

'I know you're not at all experienced in these matters and it must be a big shock to hear this . . . especially when you're busy unpacking the shopping. But right across the road from us, Dad, are enemy agents. Henry and I have had them under surveillance for days.'

The doorbell rang. 'I'd better get that,' I announced to a still stunned-looking Dad. I had this wild hope it might be Julia, suddenly released.

But it was Henry.

He blurted out, 'I want to say I'm very sorry for my behaviour yesterday and—'

'No, it was all my fault, but we haven't got time for that now.' I nodded at him to come in, and then closed the door tightly. 'We're in the middle of a major emergency and I've had to tell Dad you're a spy.'

'Why ever did you do that?' he asked, his voice all wobbly with shock.

'I really had no choice,' I began.

And then we both saw Dad hovering in the doorway. 'Now what's this, some kind of joke you two have cooked up?'

'Dad, this really is not a joke.' I turned to Henry. 'Will you let Dad check your ID?'

He hesitated.

'We haven't a moment to spare. Go on, Henry,' I cried. Something in my tone must have made Henry realize the urgency of the situation. And he promptly removed his left shoe.

'Isn't it the right one?' I murmured.

'Why can I never remember that?' Then he gave the heel of his right shoe a little tug.

Dad took the ID card from Henry and stared at it as if it were something he had to learn by heart. Then he said slowly, 'So is this some kind of club? I joined the army cadets when I was at school and we got a membership card—'

'Yes,' I interrupted. 'It's a bit like the army cadets, I suppose . . . you could say Henry is a spy cadet. The thing is, Dad, there's a major enemy agent called Mr Massingham. Henry has been watching the Baxters to see if he'll make contact with them . . . and I think he just has.'

Henry started at the news. 'Are you saying the Scorpion's across the road?'

I nodded excitedly. 'I'm pretty certain he is. A grey Volvo's been tailing me all day and—'

'But that's sensational news,' cut in Henry, practically shouting now. 'If he's over there now, that'll be superb. We must get a picture—'

'Excuse me,' said Dad, 'but I'm having some trouble following all this.'

'I thought you might,' I said kindly. 'The thing is, Dad, this is an emergency—'

'No, wait a moment,' said Dad. 'Are you saying, young man, you're involved in spying for your country?'

Henry looked away and said 'Yes' almost guiltily and then clammed up. So I filled in for him. 'Junior investigative operator is

142

his proper title. And the woman who's act-ing as his mum isn't really; she's a spy as well. His true mum and dad are off on super-secret missions, aren't they, Henry?'

Henry lowered his head. 'Yes, they're away,' he said stiffly. He clearly hated having to break his cover.

'And you think there's some sort of skul-duggery going on across the road?' asked Dad.

Henry looked up. 'There really is,' he said.

'Well, this all needs some taking in,' said Dad. 'How about if we all sit down while I make us a sandwich . . . ?'

'Oh no, there's no time for that,' I cried. 'You see, I think Massingham has kid-napped Julia.'

'What?' cried Dad and Henry in unison. Then Dad added more calmly, 'What on earth makes you think that?'

'I believe Massingham mistook her for me. You see—'

'Mistook her for you?' repeated Dad incredulously.

'Dad, will you stop interrupting and just listen?' I began, and then I let out a loud hiccup. 'Oh no, that's all I need,' I cried. I was almost in tears now, I was getting so worked up.

And I think Dad saw this because he said, 'All right, Tasha, just tell me nice and calmly why you think Julia has been kidnapped?'

I hiccupped twice and then said, all in a rush, 'Julia dressed up as me tonight to see if this grey Volvo I'd noticed followed her too. I also gave her a spy pen and told her to leave it behind if she got into trouble. Well, she should have been back home ages ago and she was supposed to have called me as soon as she got there. And what car did I see going into the Baxters' a few minutes ago? A grey Volvo! And by the bus stop I found this – my spy pen, which she was only supposed to drop in a major emergency.'

I thrust the spy pen into Dad's hand. He said, more to himself than to me, 'Your mother certainly picked the right time to be away.'

Then Henry walked to the front door. 'Sorry, but I can't waste another second talking – not with the Scorpion across the road. This is what I've been waiting for. I'll try and get Julia out too – by the way,

Tasha, does she know about my secret identity?'

'She does actually – you see . . .'

'It's all right, explanations later – I must go now.' He looked suddenly so strong and resolute; it was as if he'd changed into someone else before my eyes.

And it was then that I realized something else. It came to me like a thunderclap. Now I knew why that man laughing with the Scorpion in the photo looked so familiar. Oh, how could I have been so dense?

He looked exactly like Henry, didn't he? In fact, that man laughing with the Scorpion had to be Henry's dad. So why couldn't Henry have told me that?

Later I would have to ask him about that, but right now there was something else I had to say to him. 'You're not going to the Baxters' on your own.' Then I hiccupped and looked across at Dad. 'It'd be so brilliant if you came with us.'

Dad squinted at us both as if trying to get us into focus. Then he looked down at the spy pen still in his hand. 'You really think Julia is across the road?'

'I'd bet my life on it,' I said.

'All right,' Dad said quietly. 'Just to put your minds at rest I shall go with you and ask Mr and Mrs Baxter very politely if they've seen Julia tonight. But, Tasha, if she's not there, we'll go round to her house next and make sure she's safe. I'm not saying I believe you, but I'm not sure I like the sound of this either . . .'

'I knew you wouldn't let us down,' I cried. 'But I'm right – I know she's over there!'

'One condition though: you let me do all the talking.'

I let out another loud hiccup.

'I'll take that as a yes,' said Dad. 'Now, I've got the wrong shoes on for doing this. So while I change them I suggest you, Tasha, drink a glass of water slowly; that should get rid of your hiccups.'

Two minutes later, hiccup-free and with Dad now in his best shoes, the three of us marched across the road like a small army.

I whispered to Henry, 'Aren't you going to tell your bosses to send reinforcements and surround the house?'

'I've done it already,' he said.

'When?' I asked.

'Ah, I can move fast when I have to.'

'I don't know why you keep saying what a bad spy you are – I think you're an excellent one.'

And then Dad rang the Baxters' doorbell.

Chapter Nineteen

Tonight the Baxters took ages before opening the door, so I thought I'd use this time to give Dad a few tips. I hissed: 'Dad, if one of the Baxters pulls open a drawer, be very careful – there's probably an automatic cunningly hidden away . . .'

'Right, I'll remember that,' hissed Dad back. 'And if there's a hail of bullets when we go in, I'll also try and remember to duck.' He chuckled; we all did. But I could see that he still had a worried look on his face.

'Also, Dad,' I said, 'criminal masterminds enjoy talking . . .'

'Like someone else I know,' said Dad. He and Henry had a bit of a laughing attack after this. I suppose it was nerves.

And then the door finally opened and I could feel Dad's hand trembling slightly on my shoulder.

Mrs Baxter peered out at the solemn little group on her doorstep. 'Ah, good evening,' said Dad, sounding just like an over-friendly salesman. 'I think the weather's clearing up at last.'

'Yes, I believe it is,' said Mrs Baxter.

'Now, we think you might be able to assist us with a little problem,' went on Dad. 'Do you mind if we come in for a moment?'

'But of course,' said Mrs Baxter.

We piled into the dim, gloomy hallway, nearly falling over the suitcases waiting there.

'They're clearing out,' I muttered to Henry, who nodded but kept his head lowered, I noticed.

'Going away?' asked Dad.

'Yes, we thought we needed a break,' said Mr Baxter, who appeared at his wife's elbow. 'We're staying with some friends,' he went on in his deep voice. 'Now, you wanted us to help you with a problem?' His tone was quite friendly, but he and his wife stood together like a little wall, as if to prevent us getting in any further.

Dad gave a nervous cough. 'Julia, who's the best friend of Tasha here, seems to have vanished. We're rather worried about her actually and wondered if you'd seen her at all. She's about my daughter's height and tonight she borrowed one of Tasha's dresses and her coat as well.'

Mr Baxter, who had been raising a highly puzzled eyebrow through all of this, said, 'Well, I'm very sorry to hear about this disappearance, but I'm not at all sure how you think we can help.'

Dad leaned forward. 'Well, the thing is, Tasha thought a car was following her today. Julia, her friend, went out to see if this car would also trail her. The car was a grey Volvo – which she tells me is now parked in your garage.'

Suddenly there was a silence so intense that the chimes of their grandfather clock sounded positively deafening. Then, out of the corner of my eye, I saw something move; it seemed to just billow up out of the darkness. And I suddenly realized that a third person, standing very still in the doorway of the kitchen, had been listening to our conversation.

There was no mistaking this huge figure.

It was the Scorpion.

My face was as hot as fire now. I was scared but I was also a bit awestruck. It was like suddenly coming across Darth Vader or Cruella de Vil. I couldn't believe I was actually seeing such a famous, evil person.

I nudged Henry, but he didn't react – never even raised his head. I guessed he was very nervous. But I was a little bit disappointed in him actually. He'd seemed so fearless when we set off. Now he'd gone all timid and shy.

The Scorpion stepped forward. He was smiling – a smile which made me shudder all over. For as I looked into his eyes I felt something very powerful looking back at me: no one would be able to stand in his way. Then he looked away from me and said, 'Now, I'm the owner of the grey Volvo, but I only arrived a few minutes ago and I'm afraid I know nothing of any young lady.'

'You haven't just arrived here at all,' I began. But my voice had dried to a whisper and I was shaking.

Dad touched my shoulder, while the Scorpion gave this tiny laugh which started deep in his throat. It was one of the spookiest things I'd ever heard. 'You have obviously got my car mixed up with another – it's easily done,' he said smoothly.

'Yes, yes,' said Mrs Baxter eagerly. 'Volvos are so popular these days. I'm sure your friend will turn up. But I'm afraid we really can't help you.' I saw Dad hesitating. I sensed he wasn't satisfied with their story but was struggling to think what else to ask them. Should I take over now?

All at once Henry looked up. 'I think the time has come,' he announced, 'to tell you who I really am.' I waited for him to declare he was a junior investigative operator. Instead, with a big flourish, he removed his glasses and then stared right at Mr and Mrs Baxter. 'My hair was dark last time you saw me, but surely you haven't forgotten me.'

Mrs Baxter's mouth opened in shock but she hastily shut it again. And then it was as if a blind had been pulled over her face. It looked as blank now as the Scorpion's eyes.

'And so good to see *you* again,' said Henry in such a bitter voice as he faced Mr Baxter.

Mr Baxter's mouth was closed in a thin, hard line but I noticed his fists were clenched. Clearly they'd both seen Henry before. And the shock of meeting him again was so strong . . . well, for a second there Mrs Baxter had nearly lost it. But when had they met before? Was it on some earlier spy mission? And why had Henry never mentioned it to me?

Then, with incredible swiftness, Henry whipped out his mobile and took a photograph of the Baxters and the Scorpion before any of them knew what was happening.

'There's a picture I'll really treasure,' he said softly, but in such a mocking tone. 'And how are you both keeping? Neither of you are looking at all well actually . . . a bit tense, I'd say.'

The whole place had certainly gone very jumpy. Mr Baxter's eyes flashed. 'I'm very sorry,' he said, 'but my wife and I have never seen you before – and neither do we know anything about this missing girl.'

Then a voice said, 'I really think it's best if you all leave now.' The air seemed to shimmer with danger every time the Scorpion spoke, even though he was still smiling. In fact a smile seemed to be set on his face. There was silence for a moment while Mr Baxter pushed through us and opened his front door, just the way people do when they're letting the cat out at night.

'You haven't heard the last of this,' said Henry grimly.

'No threats please – just leave my home as you've been asked,' said Mr Baxter.

Suddenly, impulsively, I yelled out: 'Julia, Julia, are you here? Julia!'

Two things happened then. Mr Baxter hastily closed the door again, declaring, 'This is outrageous.' And I heard something fall upstairs.

Mrs Baxter's face twisted with a horrible fear. She seemed about to say something too until her husband and the Scorpion quickly surrounded her.

I saw my chance and in a flash I shot

past everyone and sprinted up the stairs three at a time. I heard Mrs Baxter let out a terrible shriek. But incredibly, no one seemed to be following me. On the landing I skidded to a halt outside the first door I saw.

It was locked, but the key was in the lock. I turned it and burst into a tiny room. The curtains were drawn and all I could see was a camp bed and a large wardrobe. Tottering by the camp bed – and looking just like a sleepwalker – was Julia.

'Oh, I am glad to see you!' I cried.

'I heard you downstairs but I couldn't get you to hear me until I bumped into that lamp.'

I gave her a quick hug, and then yelled: 'I've found Julia!'

Dad and Henry came steaming up the stairs. Dad couldn't speak when he first saw Julia; he just let out a low groan of horror and amazement. Poor old Dad, he wasn't used to such an exciting life.

'I felt something wasn't right here tonight,' said Dad. 'But what on earth has happened? Thank goodness I listened to you, Tasha . . . I never expected this.'

'Oh, I did,' I replied.

'How are you feeling, Julia?' Dad asked anxiously.

'Oh, I'm fine,' said Julia, swaying about all over the place.

'I'm very, very sorry, Julia,' said Henry.

'Why? It's not your fault,' said Julia. 'It's mine really for listening to this mad girl.'

'I suppose the Scorpion plunged a syringe into you—' I began.

'Not at all,' interrupted Julia, supported on one side by me now, and by my dad on the other. 'It's much worse than that. I saw that grey Volvo, just as you said. Then Hulky Features got out of the car – and he was the man in the photograph. For once Tasha hadn't been talking a load of total rubbish. I cried out, "Massingham," and just managed to fling that so-called spy pen away before I did a really stupid thing – I fainted. I think I must have hit my head as well.'

She half smiled at me. 'Remind me never to pretend to be you again. Anyway, I think the Scorpion must have panicked because I dimly remember him picking me up. I came round from my fainting attack here and dear Mrs Baxter was looming over me, saying she knew I was a friend of yours, and if I lay down for a bit and kept completely quiet, I'd probably be able to leave soon. Then I heard the key in the lock . . . you really have got the most charming neighbours, Tasha.'

Dad pulled out his mobile phone. 'I'm calling the police right now. Mr and Mrs Baxter – and that other very large man downstairs – have got a lot of questions to answer.'

'Where are they?' asked Henry suddenly.

It was oddly silent down there – and very surprising, too, that no one had come upstairs.

'I expect they're still looking after Mrs Baxter,' said Dad. 'She had some sort of collapse after you ran upstairs, Tasha.' He'd just started talking on the phone to the police when Henry, who'd gone to the top of the stairs, yelled, 'They're getting away.'

'What!' I gasped.

'Yeah, they're making a run for it. And they've got to be stopped.' Before anyone could reply he was already hurtling down the stairs.

'Wait for me,' I cried, tearing after him.

Henry was leaping towards the front door. The suitcases had gone from the hallway and then we saw that the Baxters and the Scorpion had opened the garage doors and were getting into the grey Volvo.

'They won't get far,' I said, 'not now Dad's called the police . . .' Then I added, 'But where are your people? They should be here by now. And why did you ask the Baxters if they recognized you?'

Henry didn't answer; in fact, I don't think he even heard me. Instead he streaked off like a bullet and threw himself in the car's path. Inspired by his awesome bravery, I pounded out beside him. He shook his head. 'No, don't, Tasha, this is my battle now.'

'I'm in this to the finish,' I replied.

The Scorpion poked his head out of the driver's seat and yelled: 'Come on, out of the way.' There was still a smile on his face, but it had hardened into a grin of fury.

'I'm not going anywhere,' Henry yelled back.

'And neither am I,' I added, just to reinforce the point.

Then the Scorpion turned the car's

headlights on to us. Of course they were dazzling, but if that was supposed to intimidate us, it didn't work. Instead we started yelling, almost as if we were willing the Scorpion to do his worst.

Our voices fell away somewhat as the car came steaming out of the garage towards us. Henry pulled me back and we dodged to the side just in time. I really believe the Scorpion would have run us over. It seemed he and the Baxters were going to get away after all. You can imagine how I felt. But I don't think you'll guess what I did next.

It was undoubtedly the maddest thing I've ever attempted. And I'm sure if I'd thought about it properly I'd never have done it.

Acting purely on the spur of the moment, I threw myself onto the boot of the car. I thought I could hang onto the sides and try climbing in through one of the windows. Instead Mrs Baxter started screaming at the Scorpion to stop. The car shuddered to a halt, sending me tumbling into the air, and then the road came rushing up at me, just before I hit it.

Most of the breath seemed to have been

jolted out of me. And I just lay there, gasping. It had all gone a bit foggy too. I do remember seeing Dad's face quite clearly for a moment. And I thought, poor Dad, he looks like a stuffed frog. He just can't take the pace.

And then there was only blackness.

Chapter Twenty

It was the pain that woke me up. My head was throbbing away, while my neck felt really stiff. And there was Dad gazing down at me again, still with a face like a stuffed frog. Also hovering around me I recognized Mrs Ventress, the local doctor.

She fussed about for ages, doing all these little tests on me. In the end I just wished she'd go because I was bursting with questions about the Baxters and the Scorpion. Several centuries passed before she finally left, and after a couple of attempts I managed to sit up and cry, 'Did the police catch the Baxters – and the Scorpion?'

'Lie down again,' said Dad firmly. 'And listen to me. It's a wonder you're not in hospital . . . jumping onto that car! I mean, what were you thinking of? It was insane . . .'

'I know all that, Dad, but have the Baxters been caught?'

He continued to ignore my questions. 'It's one thing to try and rescue your friend: that I can understand. But acting as if you're some sort of stuntwoman . . . well, I aged twenty years in that moment.'

'I'm truly sorry, Dad, and later I'll swear on a stack of Sherlock Holmes books that I'll never do anything so mind-bogglingly mad again – but you've got to tell me . . . what's happened?'

'Well, Mrs Baxter collapsed again after your little stunt. I know how she felt,' he added, 'and all three of them went back inside the house. I think they knew they'd lost. They're all at a police station now.'

'Oh, that's excellent news.' I tried to smile, only my face ached too much. 'And how's Julia?'

'Back with her parents and very worried

162

about you. She's left a message for you, by the way.'

'Oh, yes.'

'She said to tell you – and I'm quoting exactly now – you're a total wally brain.'

'That's my best friend all right.'

'Well, I second what Julia said. When you ran at the car . . .'

Not wanting to return to that topic, I asked. 'And how's Henry?'

'He's downstairs . . .'

'May I see him . . . please? It'll aid my recovery ever so much.'

'Well, just for a moment,' said Dad.

And then Henry rushed in. It was slightly weird seeing him without his glasses. He obviously didn't need to be in disguise any more. 'What you did tonight,' he cried. 'It was sensational.'

'Well, it had to be done,' I said, with what I hoped was a modest smile.

'But how exactly are you?'

'Riddled with pain but I'll bounce back . . . and I'm just so happy you caught the Scorpion and the Baxters. I bet your bosses were pleased.'

He looked away for a moment. 'Oh, yes.'

'Where were they by the way?'

'Oh, they were around,' he said vaguely.

'Well, you'll get your promotion for certain now. You pulled off that mission all right. You did a brilliant job. And you inspired me, actually. The way you stood in front of that car . . . so fearless.' I stopped. Something wasn't right. I'm very quick at sensing things like that, even when I'm recovering from performing highly dangerous stunts.

'The Baxters . . . we did capture them?' I asked.

'Oh, yes.'

'And they are traitorous enemy agents?'

He looked suddenly as awkward as when I'd first known him. 'The thing is' – there was a struggle in his voice – 'no, they're not traitorous enemy agents, I'm afraid.'

I drew my breath in sharply. 'But why aren't they?' I began.

He said quietly, 'They just aren't.'

This was a terrible blow. I looked at Henry. He was deathly pale now. 'And you are in trouble about the Baxters not being who you thought?' I asked anxiously.

There was a moment's pause before he murmured, 'There's something I've got to tell you.'

I looked at him and then said softly, 'Have you been sacked? Well, don't worry, because it's their loss. You're really good. And I know spying talent when I see it.'

He knelt down and put out his hand as though to take mine, but then he quickly drew it away again, and instead he seemed to thump the air with frustration.

'Come on, I know something's not right,' I said. 'So just tell me before I explode.'

He stood up as if he were about to recite something. Then his shoulders went back and he said in this dull, flat voice, 'I'm truly sorry but I'm afraid I'm not a spy, never have been. I made the whole thing up.'

I hadn't seen that coming at all and I said dazedly, 'But of course you're a spy. You've got to be.'

'No, I'm not!' He yelled this out in a kind of angry wail.

There was a moment of dead silence. I was just frozen by shock and dismay. Then the realization of all his many lies fell on me. It was like being touched by an icy cold hand. I shivered all over and cried out in a loud, shrill voice, 'I really believed you, Henry. I mean, I threw myself on that car thinking I was helping my country . . . and all the time it was just make-believe.' My voice rose even louder. 'You've betrayed me massively.'

'Will you just let me explain something?' he whispered.

I shook my head vigorously. The disappointment was so crushing that I couldn't bear to listen to another word. I swallowed hard to stop myself from starting to cry, but a few hot tears still rushed down my cheeks. Henry stood up in alarm.

'Oh, now look, I'm really sorry.'

And then Dad, who must have been earwigging at the door, was back in saying, 'I think you'd better go now, Henry.'

Henry said, 'I'll come back tomorrow and see you then, Tasha.'

'Don't bother,' I snapped and I could feel my face turning all hard and closed in on itself. Then I gave this odd little laugh of despair.

'She'll be calmer later,' murmured Dad.

But I wasn't. And when Henry turned up next morning I refused to see him. I wasn't at all well anyway, had a kind of reaction to the shock of what had happened. And the doctor said I must stay in bed until she called again. So the only people I spoke to – apart from Dad, of course – were Julia, and Mum on the phone from America, telling me she'd be home next week.

The rest of the day I just lay there, while this anger and frustration still burned away inside me. No doubt Henry had some kind of explanation for betraying me. But what did I care? I knew it'd be something so ordinary and deeply dull. And then I'd be thrown right back into my little life again.

Oh, why couldn't he have been a spy – even if it was a very bad one?

Why?

The following morning the doctor called again and I was allowed to totter downstairs. My legs were a bit shaky, just as they are when you first get off a fairground ride. And Dad insisted on putting a blanket over my shoulders. I felt like a really old granny. Then he said a letter had arrived for me. I knew at once by his hesitant manner who it was from.

'I'll just leave it there,' said Dad, placing it on the table beside me. 'And if you feel like reading it, that's fine. If you don't, well, no harm done.'

Henry had written me a letter. That was so strange and quaint . . . and mysterious. Part of me was intrigued. But the other part was still so furious with him for leading me on and deceiving me about something so important as being a spy.

I looked at the letter sourly. Once I nearly even ripped it into pieces, just to show how much I'd been hurt. But I had a storm of questions too. I mean, something must have been going on at the Baxters'. And why did that man – the Scorpion or whoever he was – trail me and kidnap Julia? And why . . . ?

Bursting with curiosity, I tore open the letter. But there was a massive frown on my face. I was not feeling at all generous towards Henry as I read:

Dear Tasha,

First of all I really am thoroughly sorry for what I did.

Please don't be too disappointed I am not a junior investigative operator. But that's a stupid thing to write, because I know exactly what a blow my news will be.

168

To clear up one more thing: the woman who I claimed was a spy pretending to be my mum – well, she really is my mum.

Now I have another shock for you. Last Sunday when I pretended I was having a de-briefing session with my boss, I was actually visiting my dad – in prison.

My dad used to work for a top financial company. Then one day he was approached by a man who used to work for that company too, until he got sacked. And Dad knew him vaguely. They'd even gone out on a staff outing once. You met this man earlier tonight. Let's go on calling him the Scorpion.

The Scorpion acted as if he wanted to be Dad's friend. But that was just a trick. Really he'd been planning to steal some important secrets which he knew he could sell on for a great deal of money. But he needed someone on the inside.

Dad refused immediately. But then the Scorpion said he'd found out about my dad's criminal past. It was nothing really, just a youthful indiscretion which my dad had (foolishly, as he now admits) hidden from the company.

The Scorpion threatened to reveal Dad's

secret past unless he helped him. Dad said: 'No way.' But Dad didn't tell anyone about his meetings with the Scorpion either. He hoped the Scorpion was just a big talker.

However, a few weeks later vital secrets were stolen. My dad had nothing to do with this. But evidence was cleverly planted, my dad's past was revealed – it was such a brilliant frame-up.

So my dad was found guilty of a crime he had never committed. He was certain there was someone else in the company who'd helped the Scorpion. And he strongly suspected a man there: Mr Baxter. But he claimed he'd never ever met the Scorpion. Then shortly after the break-in he took early retirement and moved with his wife to a quiet little village.

Well, you can imagine how Mum and I felt. We knew Dad was innocent and so we had to do something to help him. We couldn't just stand by. So we decided to find out exactly where the Baxters had gone. And in the end, we did.

But it wasn't until yesterday that I discovered Mr Baxter has a cousin living in Little Farthingwell called Mrs Jenkins. Mr

Baxter wanted to live here in Little Farthingwell as anonymously as possible, so he kept the link with Mrs Jenkins dead quiet. But, apparently, she knew exactly what the Baxters had done and was due to receive a cut of the money for her help.

I stopped reading here for a moment and thought, so that night in her shop, Mrs Jenkins really had been trying to warn me off when she showed me the leaflet: 'TAKE GREAT CARE.'

I read on.

Then Mum and I had our crazy idea – we'd follow the Baxters and watch for anything suspicious: for instance, if they started spending a lot of money. We knew it was a long shot, but we couldn't just stand by. We had to do something, anything, to help Dad.

So Mum rented a cottage on a short let in your village. Now, we'd both met the Baxters before. They were only very brief meetings, but to be on the safe side we used Mum's maiden name – Grimes. And Mum dyed her hair red while I dyed mine blond and wore those huge glasses. We didn't tell anyone what we were doing either. Mum said a stray word could spoil everything. Our plan must remain a secret from everyone.

Then Mum tried to subtly find out everything she could about the Baxters . . . she even compiled a little file, which is now with the police. As for me – I had to do something too. And when I found out the Baxters had a rare bird nesting in their garden, that gave me the perfect disguise: a keen bird-watcher. Except on that first night I forgot my binoculars and got run over. But one very good thing happened: by a marvellous stroke of luck I got talking to you.

Your room, Tasha, really was an ideal look-out point. Especially as we were certain the Scorpion wouldn't contact the Baxters right away with their cut of the money. No, they'd wait for the hue and cry to die down; then what better place to meet up than in an out-of-the-way village?

If we could somehow show the Baxters meeting the Scorpion, well, that would be vital evidence. Especially as they claimed they didn't know him at all.

But I couldn't keep up my pose as a bird-watcher, especially after you discovered my notebook. I couldn't tell you the truth either. So, knowing how fascinated you were by spies, I decided to become one.

It wasn't that hard. You see, I'd read a lot of the books on your shelves too. Yes, even the really old ones. You never knew that, did you? I'll tell you something else: after I told you I was a spy, do you remember how I disappeared for a couple of days? Well, I had severe doubts about going on with it – and fooling you. That's the truth.

But later, I must admit, I loved being a spy, even if it was a really bad one. Yes, I bought all those gadgets off the internet and did loads of research and I could see you believing me more and more. And soon the story started wrapping itself around me too. I didn't feel as if I were deceiving you any more. Somehow it was real.

And then I told myself it wasn't a total lie. I was actually doing some spying – just not in the way you thought.

Feel free to disagree.

And all the time I was just so desperate to catch the Scorpion at the Baxters' . . . that's why I showed you that picture of him. The only one we had. I knew I was taking a massive risk though, because the other man in the picture with him was my dad. And everyone always says how alike we are . . . well, you saw that, didn't you?

I look another huge gamble when I told you the Scorpion's name was Massingham. That's not true by the way. I was about to tell you his real name when I got worried that maybe I was putting you in too much danger – well, you've seen how nasty and treacherous he can be. So he's not called Massingham. But I am. Yeah, that's my real name: Henry Massingham.

Of course, when you said the name Massingham to the Baxters it really panicked them. They'd seen you with the listening equipment and assumed you'd overheard one of their conversations.

They went haywire then. Especially Mrs Baxter – and it was her voice, by the way, you heard on the common that night. The Scorpion apparently came down early to calm Mrs Baxter down and find out what you were up to. They even worried that you were about to try and blackmail them, you got them so freaked out.

Yes, it was the Scorpion trailing you. But

that evening, when Julia dressed up as you and then fainted, he decided life would just be safer with you out of the way until they'd left Little Farthingwell. It wasn't until he returned to the Baxters' that he realized he'd kidnapped the wrong person.

They had the money and were all set to make a very quick getaway on a plane to Spain when we turned up, just in the nick of time.

You saying 'Massingham' that night, Tasha, was actually an act of genius. It rattled them so much they started getting reckless and making serious mistakes.

But then you've been brilliant through it all. And now Mum and I are very, very hopeful that Dad's going to get a re-trial.

I hated lying to you, Tasha. Yet the truth is, I had the time of my life as well. Try and not think too badly of someone who's:

Not a spy.

Not a junior investigative operator.

But is still your friend, I hope.

Henry.

After reading that letter I wanted to ring Henry right away. Only my heart seemed to have jumped into my throat and

I could hardly speak. So in the end I sent him a text.

It said something I never, ever thought I'd write.

'Hi Henry,
   I'm very pleased you're not a spy, as your real story is the best I've ever read.
   Tasha.

Chapter Twenty-One

The following morning Henry called round. And he had one last shock for me. He was coming round to say good-bye.

He and his mum were going to London to see their lawyer. Next they were going to visit Henry's dad again and then it was back to their old home – as their work here was done.

Dad insisted on making Henry a quick snack. And I could hear Dad whistling in the kitchen as he prepared it. He said he's happy that I'm fully recovered now. But I think also he's rather proud of himself and the way he took charge of our expedition to the Baxters'. 'Not something I ever expected to do,' I heard him telling Mum on the phone. 'But well, I didn't let myself down – in fact, I think you'd have been quite proud of me.'

Later Henry came upstairs and had one last look at the surveillance look-out, also known as my bedroom. 'As soon as I walk in here I want to go straight to the window,' he said.

'So do I.' I smiled. 'And I've got to say, these last few days . . . well, I've loved having such an exciting life. My very own spy drama right here in my bedroom. Who could ask for more?' I could have added, 'My life's going to seem so much duller and greyer without you.' But I didn't, because . . . well, I just didn't. And anyway, that was only partly true. Because now it was as if I'd been through a secret door that hardly anyone knew existed. And I'd seen for myself that there was more to life than most people ever dreamed.

Henry and I sat grinning at each other. I felt so close to him that night, yet oddly shy as well.

Then he said unexpectedly, 'One thing I

feel bad about. I think I wrecked you going out with Leo.'

'You really did,' I agreed. 'But I'll get over it. And Leo already has. He's seeing Julia tonight, you know.'

'No way.' He looked astonished.

'Oh yeah. He's taking her bowling. He came round to ask my permission first, which was kind of cute. And then Julia told me she'd always liked him, but as he was going out with me she didn't think she had a chance. And do you know, I never for a second suspected that she fancied Leo. And I call myself a detective.'

Henry grinned, and then he started gazing at my shelves full of thrillers. 'I just love these stories,' he said.

'They're the best. But you and your mum giving up everything to try and save your dad from being wrongly imprisoned – well, I'd say that's even better than Sherlock Holmes and *The Man with the Twisted Lip*, or . . . or any story on my shelves.'

Henry looked pleased and embarrassed both at once. 'Don't know what to say to that . . . that's an incredible compliment.'

'It certainly is,' I agreed. 'So come on,

when do you think your dad will be freed?'

'They don't know exactly yet. Our solicitor said the Baxters have been talking their heads off at the police station, so it's got to be soon. When I saw Dad yesterday, do you know, he was like his old self – cracking jokes and everything? I just want him safely home again now.'

Then he went and stood by the window once more. 'By the way, these past weeks – working with you – well it's been immense.' Then his mobile gave two rings. 'That's my mum saying she's on her way round to pick me up . . . so I suppose I'd better be making tracks.'

'*Making tracks.*' Why did Henry always let himself down by using really un-cool phrases like that? But then I thought, What on earth does it matter? And it doesn't. It's the person behind all that surface stuff that's important: nothing else.

I said to him, 'Well, you take care, all right, and just before you go, I've got something belonging to you.'

'What's that?'

'When you were proving to Dad you were a spy, you took your membership card out of your right shoe. Remember?

'After trying my left first, yeah, I remember.'

'Well, I'm keeping it.'

'That mangy old thing?'

'I'm keeping it for a reason,' I said. 'Spies can't go very far without their ID card, can they? So you'll just have to come back for it . . .'

A slow smile spread across Henry's face.

'Oh, I'll be back,' he said.

TRUST ME,
I'M A TROUBLEMAKER
Pete Johnson

Got called a 'bod' again today. Also a 'stupid creep', a 'suck-up' and 'teacher's pet'.

Archie is twelve but sometimes he acts like he's forty! Maybe it's because he used to live with his gran. Or maybe he's just a natural nerd.

Miranda Jones, class troublemaker, is about to find out. For she's decided that she's going to change Archie – transform him from Total Loser to Troublemaker Extraordinaire.

And Archie wants her help. For surely only troublemaking can scare off Dad's ghastly new girlfriend . . .

'The devastatingly funny Pete Johnson'
Sunday Times

ISBN 0 440 86626 X

RESCUING DAD
Pete Johnson

'How do you improve your dad?'

Joe and Claire can see why Mum chucked Dad
out. He looks a mess, he can't cook and he's useless
around the house. Something must be done: they're
the only ones who can help transform him into
'Dad Mark Two'. And when they unveil this new,
improved dad, Mum will be so impressed she'll take
him back on the spot!

But then disaster strikes – Mum starts seeing the
slimy and creepy Roger. And Joe and Claire's plans
take an unexpected turn – with hilarious results.

'Pete Johnson is a wonderful story-teller'
Evening Standard

ISBN 0 440 86457 7

HOW TO TRAIN
YOUR PARENTS
Pete Johnson

They think I'M a big problem.
Wrong. THEY are!

Louis can't handle it any more. His new school is
Swotsville and his mum and dad have fallen into
some very bad ways. All they seem to care about
now is how well he's doing at school (answer: not
well) and what after-school clubs he wants to join
(answer: none!). They're no longer interested in his
jokes (his dream is to be a comedian) and have
even nicked the telly out of his bedroom!

What's going on? And can new friend Maddy
help? For Maddy tells him her parents used to
behave equally badly until she trained them.
All parents have to be trained – and she knows
a foolproof way . . .

'Peter Johnson has created a boy who makes you
laugh out loud' *Sunday Times*

ISBN 0 440 86439 9

HELP! I'M A
CLASSROOM GAMBLER
Pete Johnson

**Fool. Idiot. The very naughty boy
right at the back of the class.
That's me. Except I don't think I am bad.**

Harvey finds school stupendously, spectacularly,
mind-blowingly boring. So he decides to liven
things up a bit.

It all begins with a bet with his best mate on how
many times their maths teacher, Wobblebottom,
will scratch under his arms before the bell goes
(nine times!). And the prize is an ice cream.

But as gambling fever spreads and the bets get
bigger and bigger. Harvey suddenly finds his
genius idea has gone completely and totally . . .
OUT OF CONTROL.

'Peter Johnson has proved himself time and time
again to be an author of exceptional talents'
The School Librarian

ISBN 9 780440 866275

AVENGER
Pete Johnson

I can't ever forget what you did!
This is war now!

Gareth is thrilled when Jake, the new boy who's
full of exciting tales, befriends him — but when
Gareth is caught doing an impression of Jake's
accent, everything changes. Jake is furious and
determined to have revenge!

Gareth has to draw on the memory of his beloved
Grandad, and on the only thing he has left of him
— the magical, mysterious Avenger mask that
Grandad wore when he was a wrestler.

But is Jake really the opponent he seems to be?

'It's a brilliant read'
The Sunday Express

ISBN 9 780440 864585